WHAT THEY SAID ABOUT ONE MAN'S JOURNEY:

'It made me laugh.'
Nicola Lonsdale

'The story made me smile.'
Sue Moorcroft (Writer's Forum)

'I suggest you try looking in the Writers' & Artists' Yearbook for a publisher.'
Ian Hislop

'I am afraid that as Jonny has a full client list he has to be very careful about taking new commitments.'
Curtis Brown

'I'm afraid it's not for us.'
Anon. agent

About the author

Andrew Lonsdale was born in 1970 in County Durham. He lives in north east England.

ONE MAN'S JOURNEY

A Tale of Redemption

ANDREW LONSDALE

Copyright © 2021 A Lonsdale

The moral right of the author has been asserted.

Apart from any fair dealing for the purposes of research or private study, or criticism or review, as permitted under the Copyright, Designs and Patents Act 1988, this publication may only be reproduced, stored or transmitted, in any form or by any means, with the prior permission in writing of the publishers, or in the case of reprographic reproduction in accordance with the terms of licences issued by the Copyright Licensing Agency. Enquiries concerning reproduction outside those terms should be sent to the publishers.

Matador
9 Priory Business Park,
Wistow Road, Kibworth Beauchamp,
Leicestershire. LE8 0RX
Tel: 0116 279 2299
Email: books@troubador.co.uk
Web: www.troubador.co.uk/matador
Twitter: @matadorbooks

ISBN 978 1800462 229

British Library Cataloguing in Publication Data.
A catalogue record for this book is available from the British Library.

Printed and bound in Great Britain by 4edge Limited
Typeset in 11pt Minion Pro by Troubador Publishing Ltd, Leicester, UK

Matador is an imprint of Troubador Publishing Ltd

Thanks to Nicola and Rose.

Author's Foreword

Though this work uses the names and personae of real (whatever that means) people, it is but a work of fiction (not that I'm demoting fiction to a lower level of artistic expression, merely a side-step). The story told may allude to actual events but otherwise is entirely imagined.

Contents

Prologue	xi
Part One: A Fool's Errand	1
Banbury Cross	3
Hanging on the Telephone	10
Stand by your Man	17
This Flight Tonight	22
Waiting for my Man	26
Texas Strut	34
Sorry seems to be the Hardest Word	39
Careful with that Axe, Gordon	46
A Dose of the Motel Blues	52
Making Plans for Tony	60
The Nightmare before Lift-off	68
Life on Mars	75

Part Two: Tony on Mars	79
Into the Void	81
Deep Space Tony	89
A Day in the Life	93
Merry Xmas Everybody on Mars	99
The Pies of Wrath	104
Day Tripper	111
Two Funerals and a Wedding	117
A Single Man	124
Mars ain't the kind of Place to raise your Spirits	127
Achilles' Last Stand	130
Epilogue	135

Prologue

Oh George, thought Tony staring at the telephone, *is this really it?*

Once upon a time, he had held court amongst the empty seats at the large table in front of him, but now it seemed that his reign was almost over. Something bad was about to happen. *It already has,* he thought gloomily looking at the wooden block calendar on the table which gave the date as June 27th.

The only noise in the office was the clock on the wall facing him that was ticking loudly *...when the big hand is on the twelve and the little hand is on the one...* He closed his eyes for a moment, hoping for a different outcome when he reopened them and tried to concentrate on his one true inspiration in life: George, but instead could only imagine himself strangling someone else; someone *Scottish...*

Today, for the last time he was Tony, the destroyer of worlds. Tomorrow though, he was going to be just any old *schmoh* and that thought made him feel somewhat diminished. This day was his final one as prime minister and he still didn't know what he was going to do with himself next as the offers weren't exactly piling up. That big job at the UN hadn't materialised. The European Presidency was never going to happen, *apparently*. An ermine-cloaked trip to the House of Lords was looking increasingly unlikely. His contacts in the City hadn't come good with a top boardroom position. Even Paul McCartney had shied away from partnering him on a charity record. *His auntie's funeral, my...*

Suddenly the telephone on the table in front of him burst into life. His eyes snapped open and he lurched forward to pick up the handset. *Surely* this time it had to be George!

"Hi Tone, how's it going?" said the voice of his arch-nemesis from the earpiece.

Momentarily, the crushing disappointment that yet again, it wasn't George but rather this *Scottish nitwit,* robbed him of speech. *You're just checking to make sure I'm actually leaving, aren't you?* "Oh fine, thanks Gordon. Just tying up all the loose ends here. How's yourself and the family?"

"Oh, we're all great. Anyway, er, Tony…"

"Yes Gordon?"

"…about that knighthood I asked you about last week. I mean, I can hardly give it to myself when you've gone, can I?"

You cheeky, double-crossing… "I'll have to let you know on that one Gord as I've just been so busy. These boxes won't pack themselves. I'll give you a decision by next week sometime, maybe." In reality, Tony had already decided that he would not to issue a single gong in lieu of his resignation, so embittered was he at having been ousted from the top job in government by his *so-called* friends. Gordon especially, was not getting anything nice from him. Indeed, if Tony had anything to do with it, Gordon would be getting an *anti-gong* such as a bullet in the head or a dagger in the guts.

"Right you are then," said Gordon, "I won't keep you as I'm sure you've got lots to do. Goodbye Tony."

Yes, I have, thought Tony angrily, *like planning your bleedin' downfall.* "Yeah right Gord, see you later," he said slamming the phone down with a violent *clunk*. His shoulders tensed briefly and he slumped back into his chair with murder in mind. "Backstabber!" he said loudly. Why on Earth had he agreed to step aside for that *Scottish clown* anyway? He'd only made such a dreadful promise because he thought he could welch on it later. If only he hadn't upset all those people over that awful war business.

He put his hand inside his jacket and took out a photograph that he'd removed from its frame earlier in the *den*, where it had had pride-of-place near the treadmill. The picture showed Tony standing with an unsmiling grey-haired man next to a large pond. Wearing a fishing hat, adorned with garish fly lures, Tony was grinning inanely with his arm around the man's shoulders. *Oh George, where is that hat now?* he thought nostalgically, remembering how lucky he'd been to get the image as George didn't like being photographed.

He kissed George's image, rested the photo next to the phone and then wondered once more, what *was* he going to do with himself now? If only he hadn't made all those stupid promises. If only he had left the troops where they were. *If only, if only...* If only George would just return one of his *bleedin'* phone calls. It had been a very long time since George had actually phoned him, not like in the good old days before the Invasion when he had been on the *blower* just about every day. It seemed their relationship had cooled somewhat since Tony no longer seemed to serve any purpose for George. *Why can't he see that we could save the world together?* Was it really that wise of him to have followed George so blindly? In truth, the question never really entered his head as he was so much in love with George. The more immediate question though, was that of his next job. What the *blazes* was he going to do with himself after today?

Almost time to go, he thought watching the clock again. For the next tenant he had left something unpleasant in the upstairs toilet and he would have gone round the house and removed all the light bulbs if his beloved wife Cherie hadn't done that already. Most of their belongings had been packed away last week and taken to their new *retirement* home in the Oxfordshire countryside. The thought of retiring to the country or anywhere else for that matter filled Tony with the utmost dread.

As to his future plans, last week Tony had announced on *Newsround* that he was going to spend more time with his family and writing his autobiography. In reality, writing the *old memoirs* and spending more time with his family were the last things he wanted to do. *I'm not finished yet*, he thought determinedly watching the big hand creep onto the twelve.

Where is George? he thought staring at the phone again. *How am I going to get through all of this on my own?* Just *why* hadn't George returned any of the countless calls he had made over the last few months? Perhaps he could ring Texas one more time as George would surely want to hear his idea for a new sitcom called *Frission* set in an Iranian underground nuclear bunker.

… Mr Ahmadinejad, your mother-in-law rang…

His reveries ceased when the phone began to ring once more. *For Heaven's sake*, thought Tony, this time it *must* be George! He sat back down quickly and grabbed the handset. "Hel-lo?" he said into the mouthpiece.

"Mr Tony?" said a voice with Middle Eastern tones, "the car is ready, sir."

Fiddlesticks, thought Tony disappointedly. "I'm on my way, Jalal."

Once upon a time, Jalal had been President of Iraq in the days after the Invasion. Subsequently, things had gone a bit awry in Baghdad and when Jalal had turned up on the doorstep of Number Ten with only the clothes on his back, a battered suitcase and a sad look, Tony had felt obliged to give *the poor chap* a job. The Americans had denied him asylum because of all those completely unfounded allegations of corruption and genocide and so, feeling sorry for him, Tony had made Jalal his unofficial driver and fixer against all the advice. *Who won three elections anyway?*

With a deep intake of breath, he pushed his chair away from the desk, got to his feet and took a final long look around the office. The clock on the wall now read two minutes past one as he stared once more at the photograph of himself standing shoulder-to-shoulder with George in Texas. *Oh George*, he thought despondently, *remember me?*

Tony hesitated behind the front door leading out onto Downing Street. He could hear some awfully unpleasant noises coming from outside. Bending down to peer through the letterbox, all he could make out was the backside of the policeman standing in front of the door. Reluctantly, he straightened, placed his hand on the door handle and braced himself to open it. Why *for pity's sake* had he given up his job for that *Scottish weasel* and just what was he going to do now that everyone seemed to hate him? He fixed the best smile he could, opened the door and stepped through.

Outside the weather was overcast. Tony waved and smiled at the crowd of journalists but felt dead inside without George. Behind the gates of Downing Street, being held back by a police cordon, a large, hostile-sounding crowd could be seen waving banners.

War criminal, thought Tony indignantly as he walked towards his car. *What did these people expect? Whatever I did, I did for the good of the country.* Maintaining the smile on his face became a real struggle. *And for George.*

He had been offered the chance to make a final speech from the doorstep of Number Ten but had declined the opportunity as he hated speaking to the media now that he seemed to be so unpopular with the *proles*. Saying less and getting out quick was probably the best option, what with all that absurd talk of war crimes and trials.

Keep smiling, Tony, he said to himself as he gave a brief wave and got into the back of his car. The Jaguar then pulled away bound for the House of Commons where Tony was to make his final speech to MPs as prime minister.

"Remember, Mr Tony," said the driver, "if they ask you any questions just say that you can't remember anything."

"Er…" said Tony uncertainly.

As the car neared Parliament Square, Tony mopped his brow with a handkerchief and looked at George's image again to fortify his spirits. *Oh George*, he thought with a tear in his eye, *didn't we almost have it all?*

Meanwhile back in Downing Street, as the final members of the press departed, a removal van pulled up outside Number Ten. Inside the vehicle was a group of cleaners, the spearhead of the new tenant's private army who had been tasked to thoroughly cleanse the house of any trace of its most recent occupants. Now, the only reminder that Tony had ever lived in the prime minister's official residence, was the portrait of him gurning inanely on the stair hallway wall and something nasty bubbling away in the upstairs toilet cistern.

Part One

A Fool's Errand

I

Banbury Cross

Head bowed, Tony was standing at a lectern amid the rubble of what had once been Downing Street. Looking up slowly, he swallowed and said, "Ladies and gentlemen, members of the press, I am sure that you are all relieved that I am your prime minister again." Taking a handkerchief from his pocket he wiped away a tear. "Gordon and all the ministers who perished in the explosion were like family to me. We will never cease in our efforts to catch the perpetrators of this heinous deed."

Before long he was waving to huge crowds lining the roadside from an open-top double-decker bus as it drove through London. *All worship me*, he thought happily.

Soon he could hear his name being called, *Tony, Tony, Tony...* He closed his eyes and breathed in deeply to capture the moment but then strangely, the noise of the crowd became one voice, *"Tony..."*

"What?" he said blinking as the light around him darkened. For a moment he didn't know where he was, but then looked around and realised much to his disappointment that he wasn't crossing Waterloo Bridge in a victory bus after all but rather, was in the bedroom of his house in *delightful* Oxfordshire. His adoring multitudes had morphed into a dark-haired woman in a long pink dressing gown shaking him by the arm.

"Tony…" said his beloved wife Cherie scowling down at him.

"Wake me up in a couple of hours, dearie."

"…there's a telephone call for you. Pick up the receiver on your side."

His eyes snapped open. *Maybe*, this time it would be George! He rolled over quickly and grabbed the handset at the side of the bed. "Yes?" he said excitedly into the mouthpiece.

"Tony darling, Selwyn here…" said the voice of his agent down the line.

Oh, what now? thought Tony drearily. *Another potential guest appearance on Countdown…?* Since leaving politics, Tony had decided upon show business as a potential career avenue, so he had appointed a theatrical agent, *Selwyn Corbett Associates* to represent him. Even after a year now though, the agent (who had been recommended to him by a Tory friend who said that he'd got her on *Strictly…*) had been next to useless. Tony had been expecting at least some interest from Hollywood but so far, the only thing had been a screen test co-hosting a revival of *It's a Knockout* with a rodent puppet. The project was later shelved, indefinitely apparently because the producers felt that the host-pairing "lacked chemistry".

That bleedin' rat, thought Tony clenching his fists in rage.

"…I've got some good news for you…"

Tony's anger suddenly evaporated and he could almost hear his name being called … *and the winner of the Academy Award for …*

"…I've got this friend who works at ITV…"

… I'd like to thank one man…

"…and he's said that they're working on a new *An Audience With…* programme."

"Oh, I'd love to do it," said Tony immediately, "but I'll need a bit of help with the song and dance numbers."

"Er, sorry Tony," said his agent hesitantly, "but you'd only be in the audience."

Fiddlesticks. "I knew that," said Tony trying hard not to sound disappointed.

"The real star is going to be John Barrowman. Can I say you're interested then?"

"Erm, I guess."

"Fantastic. I'll be in touch." *Clunk.*

Bother, he thought angrily. Just who were these *peasants* to be phoning him, *Tony*, whenever they felt like it and what if George had been trying to call at the same time? He slumped back in bed, pulled the duvet over his head and shut his eyes tightly. Just what did John Barrowman have that he, *Tony*, didn't? How much more humiliation could the world heap upon him? He felt even more diminished than ever now. In reality, he was still *former* prime minister Tony Blair, currently unemployed and living in *idyllic* Oxfordshire.

Just *what* though was he going to do with himself today? Getting up held little appeal as he had nothing to do other than lolling about the house all day waiting for the phone to ring. What *had* happened to all the power and respect that he used to hold? All those dreams he'd had growing up, whilst at public school and after leaving Oxford, filled his mind like unrealised ghosts. Now it seemed like *only* ever being prime minister would be the pinnacle of his career, but would it be enough? The thing he missed the most was fêting famous people from the running machine in the den in Downing Street. Nowadays, the only time he ever saw a celebrity was on the telly or in one of his wife's dreary magazines.

Maybe George would *actually* ring this time. *No*, he knew he couldn't rely on George anymore. He must have phoned Texas over a hundred times this week already and George hadn't even called him back once. According to George's mother who usually answered the telephone, George was either working away from home, on the toilet, out jogging, having a sleep, in an important meeting, in Washington, at a dairy farmer's conference or just too *darned* busy to come to the phone. *Oh George*, thought Tony adoringly, *always devoting your time to others.*

The thought of George's greatness all became too much for him so he got out of bed, donned his snow leopard pelt dressing gown and snakeskin slippers, gifts from the people of Kazakhstan and walked over to the bay window. The sight of the English countryside in full bloom brought him no succour as he felt cold and empty inside without George. *Oh George*, he thought miserably looking towards the distant hills, *rescue me from this Hell.*

On the subject of Hell, his thoughts drifted to his old constituency in County Durham from which he'd resigned in a speech at Trimdon Colliery Club just after leaving Number Ten. He remembered how it was at that same club that he'd been chosen as a Labour candidate many years ago. *What gullible fools,* he thought contemptuously. *Maybe, I should have stayed on there. The idiots would have probably let me do the job from down here.*

Scraping noises below interrupted his reminiscing and looking down, he made out the figure of his gardener Mr Ho, turning over some flowerbeds with a spade. Ho, a Vietnamese immigrant spoke very little English but had been recommended by Cherie's friend, Carole. Tony wasn't sure if Ho had all the right papers and what not, but he was a *damned* good worker and mightily cheap to boot. Tony tapped on the window but when Ho looked up, he averted his gaze and moved hurriedly away around the side of the house. *Don't these peasants know how important I am?* thought Tony, annoyed not to have been acknowledged. *How important you used to be*, said another voice in his head.

With a deep sigh he closed the curtains and got back into bed. *Oh George,* thought Tony, forlornly looking at the phone, *wherefore art thou?* Perhaps though, George had merely lost his number and that was why he hadn't returned his calls. Maybe, all he needed to do was to ring George again right now and everything could be made better. Tony was desperate to ask George what he thought about a new quiz show he had thought up called *Win a Job*, whereby members of the proletariat would try and win some kind of gainful employment. At least, George couldn't be any less enthusiastic than Selwyn Corbett had been.

I'm sorry Roy but the position of sewer cleaner needs another 100 points…

However, instead of phoning George he opened the drawer under the phone and removed a shiny metal object that Jalal had acquired for him from *a bloke down the pub* last week. Apparently, it was something called a *Glock* and not the Walther PPK he'd requested but it was all the village arms dealer had in stock. W*here was the safety again?* The idea of using it on Gordon had occurred to him and he was considering inviting his former chancellor over for tea one afternoon. *Right between the eyes.* Latterly though, he had thought about shooting himself but was a bit worried that it might hurt.

Feeling enlivened by thoughts of murder, he got up again and went and stood in front of the long mirror by the window. He put the pistol down the side of the waistband of his Union Jack underpants and stared intently at the reflection with his hand poised above like a gunslinger from the old West. "The name's Blair, Tony…"

He reached for the gun but mistimed the action and the *damned thing* went off in his hand. He dropped the weapon immediately and wrapped his arms around his head.

"Tony!" said Cherie rushing in from the bathroom. "What on Earth was that?"

"Er, nothing dearie, just the radio I think…" said Tony. It was then that the waves of pain hit him. He looked down at his slippered left foot and noticed a dark red liquid bubbling through a hole in the leather above where his big toe used to be. "But, er, could you call for the doctor please, dearie," was the last thing he said before collapsing on the floor and passing out.

II

Hanging on the Telephone

Dear George... typed Tony from the computer in the gym-cum-office of his house in *glorious* Oxfordshire.

"Tony," said a voice from the doorway.

"Er, what dearie?" said Tony not looking up from the screen.

"Tony," repeated his beloved wife Cherie, "are you listening to me?"

Slowly he turned to look at her. "Er, yes dearie?"

"I'm off into Banbury to have some colonic therapy with Carole."

Good riddance.

"I'll be back in a couple of hours. Get chef to heat up a pie for dinner..."

Bleedin' rancid... thought Tony suddenly feeling nauseous. On leaving Number Ten, Cherie had started a business selling frozen pre-packed meat pies, hoping to ape the success of Linda McCartney. The pies were labelled as home-made and traditional British but in reality, were shipped in frozen from a factory in East Asia. Unfortunately, the business was presently foundering apparently because of the adverse taste of the pies.

"...and please, try not to shoot yourself again."

"Yes dearie," said Tony happily watching her leave. It had been just over a fortnight since the *accident* and a week since he'd returned home from the hospital. The surgeon had managed to save most of his big toe but his foot was still heavily bandaged. There had been some good news though. His agent had phoned him in the hospital and mentioned that Channel Five were looking to cast for a new television production of *The Shining* and had recommended that he read the book. A paperback lay next to the phone with a photograph of Jack Nicholson going mad with an axe on the front cover. After a deep sigh, he picked it up and opened the first page.

Stephen King was born in Portland, Maine...

Just then the telephone on the desk rang. In an instant Tony dropped the book, surged forward and grabbed the handset. *Really*, after all this time it *had* to be George!

"George?" he said eagerly into the mouthpiece.

"Tony?" said a voice quite unlike George's. "Prescott here, how are you doing me old mate?"

Oh no. "Oh hi John," said Tony trying very hard to sound unflustered. "We're all fine here, thanks. How's yourself and Pauline?"

"Look Tony, I'll get straight to the point. I've got this police report on my desk and I thought I would speak to you first in case the press gets wind of it."

"Oh?" said Tony, feeling his big toe starting to ache.

"You see Tony, an explosive device has been found in one of the toilets in Number Ten."

Crumbs, thought Tony feeling dark clouds gather around him. "No?" he said trying to sound outraged. "A bomb? That's terrible. How has this happened?"

"After Gordon took over from you, he hired this plumber to fix one of the toilets in Number Ten because he was dissatisfied with the strength of the flush in the upstairs shitter. Well, this plumber guy had a good rummage around and found a whole load of what turned out to be plastic explosive in the toilet cistern. I've only just received the report from Scotland Yard and it's not fun reading. According to the bomb experts, the explosives were so old and rotten that they could never have gone off anyway."

Fiddlesticks, thought Tony, thinking that was the last time that he would ever trust Jalal with anything important. "Oh, what a relief. If anything had happened to Gordon or yourself then I would have been heart-broken. Have the police got any leads yet?"

"Well, there's the rub, Tony," said Prescott. "You see, this report is saying that your fingerprints were found all over the explosives and the detonator."

"Oh erm," said Tony swallowing and loosening his necktie, "er, it must be from that time I tried to fix the toilet myself and I put my hand in the cistern and had a good feel about. It wasn't flushing that well even when I lived there, you know, what with Cherie and those crazy diets she's always on."

"Right," said Prescott sounding sceptical. "Anyway, I'm sure we can have a chat about it when you come down here tomorrow."

"Tomorrow?" said Tony nervously, "but, er, I've got an important speech to write for my foundation. I can't just drop everything like that." He tried to calm himself down, "Look John, I'm an incredibly busy man, you know that." In truth, he had nothing much to do. His last gainful employment had been a motivational speaking tour which had been cancelled eight months ago because of poor ticket sales. He now spent most of his time watching videos of past glories and pining for George to phone him.

"The car will be there for you at ten thirty in the morning sharp. Bye Tony." *Clunk.*

"Judas!" said Tony, slamming down the phone. He slunk back in his chair and shut his eyes from where he could imagine himself murdering Prescott with an axe, Jack Nicholson-style. How dare that working-class *clown* accuse him, *Tony*, of what practically amounted to terrorism? *And he smells worse than Gordon.*

Despairing thoughts began to cascade through his head. *How did that Scottish snake-in-the-grass ever get my job?* He'd never felt so alone and abandoned as he did right now. *Public opinion,* he thought venomously, *who cares? I wish I'd started World War Three after all. It would have served them right. Iraq would have seemed like a tea party in comparison.*

Trying to steady himself, he focussed on the one true inspiration in his life, George. *Oh George*, thought Tony removing the photo taken in Texas all those years ago from his jacket pocket, *how great thou art*. He looked into George's sombre eyes once more, *like deep mountain pools,* and felt a whole lot better.

Just then the phone rang again. *Finally*, at last, this time it had to be George. "Hel-lo?" he said into the mouthpiece.

"It's me," said his beloved wife Cherie.

"I thought you were going into Banbury."

"We're not going now. Carole's just texted me to say that the therapist has gone down with food poisoning. He's blaming my pies and says he's going to sue us."

"Really?"

"Yes really, do you think I'm making this up?"

"No dearie."

"Look Tony, have you phoned your friends in London yet about shifting all these pies? We've got ten thousand sitting in the garage and another fifteen thousand coming next week. We need to start getting rid of them."

"Yes dearie, I'll get on to it later."

"Yeah right." *Clunk*.

Tony sighed, feeling he had more important things to worry about than pies. *A car is coming tomorrow.* He got up out of his seat, limped over to the treadmill on the other side of the gym and gave it a gentle pat. He remembered running on it in Downing Street whilst conversing with the great and powerful and how the fate of nations was decided with the stroke of a pen or the push of a button or sometimes even just a telephone call, but the memories all felt so hollow now that he seemed so friendless. Sadly, Central Asian dictators just couldn't compare with the likes of George. *Oh George*, he thought forlornly, *time will prove us right.*

He looked up at the ceiling and saw a small metal hoop on which a punch bag usually hung, then stooping down he picked up a blue cable from the floor near the treadmill. *Crumbs,* thought Tony straightening, staring hard at the skipping rope in his hands, *has it really come to this?* He wheeled the swivel chair over from the computer desk, stood on it and threaded the rope through the punch bag hoop until he had made a simple noose. "Goodbye cruel world," he said placing his head inside, making sure that the rope fit snugly around his neck. *Oh George*, he thought as he kicked the chair away, *we'll meet again in heaven.*

He waited for a moment and then opened one eye to see what the afterlife looked like. Unfortunately, he seemed to be still alive and hanging excruciatingly by the neck from a skipping rope in the gym of his *retirement* home in *darkest* Oxfordshire. *Shouldn't I be dead now?* he thought disappointedly.

Suddenly the phone rang. Maybe, this time it would be George! He tore at the rope with his fingers but lacked the strength to extricate his head from the noose. He kicked wildly with his legs but the chair was agonisingly just too far away. He could feel his mind fading and his body felt very weak and light.

Just then the gym door opened and in stepped his beloved wife Cherie, reading from a piece of paper. Not seeing Tony straight away, she said, "Have you seen the size of this phone bill that's just come…?" Her last word trailed off when she looked up and saw her husband hanging from the ceiling.

"The phone!" wheezed Tony whose face was now the colour of beetroot. "Get the phone!"

His wife though, just stood there as if frozen, too shocked by the awful scene in front of her to react but then the hoop in the ceiling worked itself free and Tony, along with the rope and a large part of the ceiling, fell to the floor.

Cowboys, thought Tony with disgust, as he lay spread-eagled on the floor, covered in white ceiling debris. *That's the last time I ever trust any more of Jalal's builder friends.* He began coughing with all the dust.

"What on Earth were you thinking of, Tony?!" screamed Cherie.

A pale white Tony made no reply as he crawled painfully over ceiling fragments towards the still-ringing telephone. Eventually, he reached the desk and pulled himself up onto his knees. He outstretched his fingers and picked up the handset. "Yes?" he said feebly into the mouthpiece.

"Yo Blair," said an American voice down the receiver, "former president George W Bush here. How are you doing buddy? Laura and I were wondering if you and Cherie would like to come over to the ranch for a visit some time soon. I've got something I want to run by you."

No response came because at that moment Tony had lost consciousness caused by a combination of oxygen deprivation, surprise and total ecstasy.

III

Stand by your Man

It was just after noon as the Sun shone through the bedroom window of the Blairs' home in *glorious* Oxfordshire. Tony was sat up in bed, thinking of all the things he was going to say to George when they met up next week. Until recently, he had spent his retirement in a dark place but now all that had changed. For the first time in *aeons*, he was feeling optimistic about the future. *Oh George*, thought Tony looking down at the silver tea tray on his lap, *together we're unstoppable.*

Resting on the tray was a white envelope. Jalal had already binned all the junk mail from the families of dead service-personnel, leaving a single letter post-marked *Texas, USA*. Trying to savour the moment, Tony opened the envelope carefully with an ornate letter opener and holding the freshly-cut aperture up to his nose, inhaled strongly. He trembled inside and thought giddily, *Oh George...*

Unfortunately, the letter of invitation was rather brief, merely stating in typed lettering the arrival and exit times from George's house in Texas and nothing about the specific purpose of the visit. Most disappointedly of all, it said nothing about how much George loved him. At least though, George had stamped it, *best wishes George.*

Tony held the letter to his breast, closed his eyes and thought about the bright future that now awaited him. He was certain that George had a top job lined up for him: George's man at the UN, Secretary General of NATO or maybe even some kind of Middle-East peace-making role. *Oh George,* though Tony ecstatically, *side by side once more.*

His beloved wife Cherie had made all the travel arrangements as Tony still couldn't speak properly given his recent *accident*. The Blairs were flying to Houston from Heathrow next Tuesday, first class of course and from there were being taken to George's ranch in Crawford, Texas where they would stay for two nights.

Tony had arranged for Jalal to look after the house while they were gone. He had originally wanted Jalal to come along on the trip, but the US Embassy had refused to issue him with a visa because of those ridiculous genocide rumours still hanging about. *The poor chap was only following orders*. He mused that Jalal was probably his only friend left in the world now. Cherie was hardly ever nice to him and the Labour Party seemed embarrassed to be associated with him. *Well*, he would be seeing George very soon so *they could all go to Hell!*

He blinked and rubbed the nasty weal on the side of

his neck. Last night, he had gone out with Jalal to meet some Iraqi businessmen in the village pub and he'd been forced to wear one of his wife's scarves around his neck in order to hide the mark. At least the meeting had been successful as twenty five thousand of *Mrs Blair's Olde English Country Pies* and *Mrs Blair's Finest Pork Pies* were about to be loaded into an RAF Hercules for the starving in war-torn Baghdad. It was because of this deal that he was now back in Cherie's good books. She had forgiven his suicide attempt and had even promised him something other than one of her pies for tea tonight.

Now feeling much more like his old confident self, he put the tray on top of the bedside cabinet and got out of bed. Donning his dressing gown and slippers he went over to the long mirror by the window. "Colleagues," he said to his reflection, "I stand by my decision to intervene..." *Oh George*, he thought happily, *shoulder to shoulder again.* "Ladies and gentlemen, members of the committee; this peace prize really belongs to one man..."

Just then the door opened and in walked his beloved wife Cherie eating a pie. "Talking to yourself again Tony? I thought the psychiatrist had sorted that one out? At least we can all be grateful that you weren't trying to hang yourself again."

"Look dearie," said Tony tetchily, "I'm just trying to get into the swing of things for when we see George next week."

Cherie grimaced sarcastically and took another bite of her pie, "Anyway, Carole's just phoned to say our crystal pendants are ready to pick up. They'll protect us all from any negative karmic energy out there. Make sure that you wear yours. I'll be checking."

Stick it up your… "Yes dearie."

"What do you think George wants anyway?" said Cherie chewing on some gristle. "I thought he'd got bored with you a long time ago."

"Oh Cherie, don't be ridiculous. Me and George, we're like that." said Tony crossing his fingers and winking. "I think he's going to offer me a top job."

"Whatever. Anyway, it's pie for tea tonight. I'm afraid Jalal couldn't get into town today for any groceries."

"Why on Earth not?" said Tony, sick to the guts of her pies.

"He's taken to his bed ill with what he says is food poisoning from my pies but I think that's a bit unlikely."

"No, of course not, dearie."

"Anyway, Carole will be over soon with the vitamin enemas so if you must kill yourself, keep the noise down."

Go and… "Yes dearie."

When she'd gone, he got back into bed and read George's letter again. *Oh George*, he thought admiringly, *you always knew what to say*. Then he put the letter back on the tray and from the bedside cabinet drawer removed the photograph of himself with George in Texas. George's phlegmatic eyes gazed back at him from the picture and he realised that the only truth worth knowing lay within the gift of one man. However, as he looked upon George's image, it entered his head that it was all a bit odd that he always managed to call when George had just popped out to the shops or was unavailable because of an earthquake or was busy helping the underprivileged and was never able to call him back. *Oh George,* he thought, keying the now-familiar number into the dial-pad of the bedside phone, *always helping those worse off.*

IV
This Flight Tonight

Tony was sat in the economy class section of a large airliner. He stared blankly ahead at the head-rest of the seat in front of him and fingered a rough crystal of purple quartz that was hanging from his neck by a silver chain. The pendant was said to be able to ward off bad luck and had cost thousands of pounds. *Cobblers,* thought Tony.

He could remember from national security meetings how vulnerable civilian airliners were to sabotage, terrorism or just mechanical issues. The days when he used to have a plane at his own disposal were sadly long gone. *Just keep staring straight ahead, Tony,* he thought breathing deeply.

He tightened his seat belt when the warning light came on and checked to feel if the flowery scarf around his neck was still in place. The plane juddered to a start, taxied down to the end of the runway and fired its engines. *It's safer than crossing the road*, thought Tony gripping the arm-rests tightly, feeling the aircraft leave the ground. *Flying coffins,* said another voice in his head.

Ten minutes later when the plane had reached its cruising altitude, the hazard lights clicked off. Tony removed his seatbelt and gave a sigh. *Negative karmic energy my…*

"Hey buddy," said a large, besuited middle-aged man, sitting in the seat next to him. "Aren't you that prime minister fellow from Great Britain?"

Oh no. "Er, used to be," said Tony.

"Well, it's very nice to meet you, friend. My name is John Kuppernickel and I'm originally from Minnesota, USA. I sell screws, washers and nuts," said John Kuppernickel who then reached across and gripped Tony's hand with what felt like a vice of steel.

Just who are you…? "Er, nice to meet you, Tony Blair," said Tony trying not to wince from the tight handshake.

"Here's my card Mr Blair or may I call you Tony?"

Tony accepted the card as if was infected with plague. "Er, yes Tony's, er, fine, I suppose," said Tony, noticing a flight attendant walking down the aisle towards him. "Stewardess, stewardess," said Tony frantically waving his arms about in order to attract her attention.

"Yes sir?" said the woman stopping at his seat.

"I was told I could move up to the front once the plane was at cruising altitude. Is there any chance of going now?" Because of a booking error Tony was sat at the back of economy class whilst his beloved wife Cherie and the bodyguards were all in first.

"I'm sorry sir, but you've no hope now. This plane is completely full."

"Oh bother," said Tony out aloud.

"Never mind buddy," said John Kuppernickel patting him heavily on the shoulder, "I'll keep you company. The flight's only another nine hours anyway. I fly long-haul regularly and all you have to do is make a game of it. I find that if you count how many times the stewardesses walk past every hour and then try and break that record in the next hour, the time just flies by."

I wish I was dead, thought Tony miserably, o*r rather you were.*

"Do you know what, Tony? I'm a big fan of that Brown fellow. He seems to know how to get the job done. Are you two really such good buddies?"

Tony rubbed the crystal again. "Sorry John, but do you mind," he said fetching a book from his jacket pocket, "I'm trying to finish this."

"No problem-o, Tony. Don't mind me. My wife says I talk too much. I'll just sit back and let you get on."

Finally, thought Tony settling back into his seat to read.

Stephen King was born in Portland, Maine…

"Which one is your favourite?" said Kuppernickel staring at Tony's book.

"Er, sorry?" said Tony.

"Mine is *The Dead Zone*, but I have a soft spot for *Salem's Lot*."

Tony, who really disliked reading, was almost lost for words. "Er…"

"Some people say that his later work is not up to scratch…"

Of all the people on the plane, thought Tony cursing his luck.

"… but I just love the *Dark Tower* series."

Tony began rubbing the pendant again. *Please work and make him shut up.*

"Now, Tony I stay in lots of hotel rooms and the only book that gives me solace other than those written by Mr King, is the good book itself. How about you?"

"Er…"

V
Waiting for my Man

Bleedin' pendants, thought Tony angrily sat in the back seat of the black SUV as it left the airport. *Total utter codswallop.* He was not a happy man. *Nearly fifteen hours of non-stop waffle.* The plane's arrival into Houston had been delayed because of a mechanical issue which had resulted in its grounding in Canada for an extra five hours. *If it wasn't about screws or washers then it was stupid horror stories or Jesus.* And then just before passing through customs, John Kuppernickel had invited Tony and family over to his home in Minnesota "any time you like, buddy". *Fat chance of me ever going within a thousand miles of his stinking house.* His mood began to lighten though as the Hummer sped along the freeway that led to George's home.

It was about one thirty in the afternoon when the car pulled up outside the mock-Tudor mansion where the Bushes resided when they were in Texas. A gardener, trimming roses in the front garden, stopped working and covered his eyes to see who had just arrived. As the vehicle drew to a halt, the rear window rolled down and a beaming tanned face could be seen looking out.

Oh George, thought Tony, full of joy in the back seat, *thy people shall be my people.* As soon as the car stopped, he opened his door and leapt out. The gravel crunched under his feet as he took a good look around, fondly remembering his first visit long ago when George had been there to meet him on the drive. Disappointingly though, there was no sign of George today. In the days before the Invasion, George had been much easier to reach than now, but with George's recent phone call and letter, Tony was certain that their relationship had turned a corner for the better. George, *surely* was somewhere close-by.

The front door of the house opened and out stepped an old, white-haired woman in a blue dress followed by a middle-aged woman wearing jeans. Tony knew who they were from previous meetings: Barbara, George's mother and Laura, George's wife.

"Welcome back to McLennan County, Tony. Thanks for popping over," said Barbara embracing him whilst Laura hugged Cherie. "George will be pleased that you're here safe and sound."

"Er, where is George?" asked Tony.

"Oh, he's had to pop over to Florida on business for a day or two. He asked Laura and me to make you all as comfortable as we can until he gets back."

"Oh right," said Tony unable to hide the extreme disappointment in his voice.

"Anyway," said Barbara, "how was your journey here?"

One of the worst. "Oh, not too bad," said Tony.

"We heard you had a bit of trouble at the airport, Cherie." said Laura.

"All my clothes and beauty stuff have disappeared," said Cherie tearfully.

"Er, yes," said Tony remembering the huge flare-up between his beloved wife and the customs officials about what had happened to their cases. Apparently, Johannesburg was the likeliest destination.

"Well, I'm sure it could have happened to anyone," said Barbara. "Don't worry Cherie, Laura has got some things that you can wear and Tony, George has got plenty of clothes that'll fit you. Then tomorrow, we can all go down to the local mall and pick you up some new threads."

"You see dearie," said Tony to Cherie, "I told you we'd manage."

"Just get the hand luggage, Tony."

Yes, my lady. Tony limped over to the rear of the car and removed a small case from the boot. "Here you are, dearie," he said, out of breath from the effort.

"Tony and I have brought you a present over from England," said Cherie enthusiastically.

"Oh my," said Barbara. "You shouldn't have."

"It's no bother," said Cherie opening the case to reveal a white cardboard box.

Really, it's not, thought Tony.

"Well, thank you very much," said Barbara looking inside the box. "It appears to be some uncooked pastries,"

"Not just any old pastries," said Cherie. "These are traditional home-made British meat pies from my premium range. They're absolutely delicious."

"What? You made them yourself? That's just fantastic," said Barbara. "You know I try and bake as often as I can for George senior, but I'm usually just too *darned* busy."

"Er, oh yes, it's an old family recipe," replied Cherie.

"I'll get chef to prepare them for tonight's meal. I can't wait to taste that home-cooked English flavour," said Barbara. "Now why don't y'all come into the house and make yourselves comfortable after your long journey."

"Erm," said Tony, desperate to avoid eating any more of Cherie's pies, "er, wouldn't it be better if we waited for George to come back first before we…"

"Nonsense Tony," said Barbara taking his arm. "Why, George won't mind a bit. I'll get Chef to freeze any leftovers for when George gets back so he doesn't miss out. He just adores pastries."

He won't after one of these, thought Tony grimly.

That evening, Tony was sat at a large wooden rectangular table with Cherie, Barbara and Laura in the Bushes' dining room. Before coming down for dinner he'd changed out of his travelling suit into an old brown tracksuit belonging to George that was in the wardrobe in his room. *Gosh,* he thought wearily, looking at the greyish brown pastry on the plate in front of him, *I'm really sick of these revolting things.*

"So Cherie," said Barbara chewing awkwardly on some gristle, "just what kind of meat is in these pies?"

"Only the finest organic English beef."

"Really?" said Barbara. "It has a most unusual taste. I could have sworn it was something I'd never tried before."

Like Alsatian. "Anyway Laura," said Tony, "did George tell you why he's invited us over here?"

"Excuse me for a second," said Laura spitting something into her napkin. "I'm afraid not Tony, I look after the family home whilst George does, well, whatever George does. He usually doesn't tell me many details, but this time he did say that he had a really big job lined up for you."

Tony almost choked on his wine at this revelation, "Oh well, that's great. One has so many commitments at home but any new opportunities will be given the fullest consideration."

"Just how have you been filling in your time, Tony since you resigned as prime minister?" asked Barbara leaning over and touching him on the back of the hand.

"Oh, this and that you know. Some of it's so hush-hush that I'd have to shoot you if I told you," said Tony laughing at his own joke.

"Oh really?" said Barbara. "You must tell me all about it when you can."

Gosh, thought Tony, bored to death, *just where is George?* "Will do," he said chipperly.

"I hate to ask you Tony," said Barbara in a concerned manner, "but how is poor Gordon Brown getting along since the election? The reports we've been receiving over here about his state of mind are very pessimistic."

I've got a spare skipping rope at home. "Oh, it's absolutely terrible," said Tony putting on his saddest face. "I've been on the phone every day to him. Gordon is such a good friend to me and my family. He is our rock in stormy times. I just don't know how the country will manage without him."

"Oh my, my, you poor man," said Barbara sympathetically. "You must pass on my best wishes to Gordon and his family."

"Yes of course," said Tony as sincerely as he could manage.

"You know Laura," said Cherie, "the US distribution rights for Mrs Blair's Olde English Country Pies are still up for grabs…"

Tony aimlessly gnawed on some pie crust whilst his wife tried to interest the Bushes in her pastries. He scratched his thigh and felt a lump in one of the trouser pockets. He put his hand inside and removed a small brown mass. He realised immediately what it was as he recognised the odour from his days at university. *Crumbs!* he thought in a panic, *someone's trying to plant something on George.* As surreptitiously as he could manage, he threw the lump towards the burning log fire near to him. Unfortunately, it only hit the surround and bounced back to land on the marble hearth. Before he could react though, a small brown and white dog appeared from the shadows and swallowed it whole.

As this was happening, a large man in servant's livery appeared in the room. "There's a telephone call for you, Mrs Bush," said the man. Tony immediately recognised the voice as being that of George's butler who often answered the phone when he rang. "It's your eldest son, Mr Bush. He wishes to speak with you."

"Thank you Cheeseborough," said Barbara getting up from her seat. "Please, excuse me everyone," and with that she left the room followed by the butler.

While this was happening, Tony lowered the remnants of his pie under the table and waved it in the direction of the small dog. The dog walked over slowly and after sniffing the pie once, grabbed it out of his hand and began to eat it under the table.

Result, thought Tony jubilantly.

"More pie anybody? said Laura turning towards the Blairs.

Not bleedin'… "No thank you," said Tony who was still ravenously hungry, "I'm already so full, I wouldn't be able to eat my dessert. What is for afters anyway?"

"Oh, I think its Chef's speciality," said Laura, "courgettes in a lemon sauce served in a giant Yorkshire pudding."

Yak! "Mmm," said Tony, "sounds scrummy."

"Actually Laura," interjected Cherie. "I'm sure Tony would love another pie."

"Er, no dear, I'm just about full up, thank you."

"No, I insist. In fact, get him two please Laura. He is just being modest. He absolutely adores them really."

"Of course, Cherie," said Laura leaving for the kitchen.

"I didn't want any more of your *rancid* pies," hissed Tony at Cherie. "There's absolutely nothing worse."

"Just make the effort, Tony. I saw you feeding that dog," said Cherie. "If we can tie up this deal, we'll be off the hook for the pie contract. There's a hundred thousand of the bloody things nearing Thames Dock sometime soon and not one retailer back home is…"

"Well everyone," said Barbara jauntily as she returned to the table, "you'll be pleased to learn that George is coming back home tomorrow. He'll be here in the morning and he said that he's got a nice surprise for you, Tony."

For a moment Tony was unable to speak such was his happiness. *Oh George*, he thought with joy in his heart, *arm in arm once more.*

"Here's your food Tony," said Laura returning from the kitchen carrying a plate.

Food? thought Tony feeling his ecstasy fade at the sight of the pastries in front of him. "Oh great," he said without much feeling. *Where's that pooch?* he thought, looking around the room, but unfortunately, the dog had vanished.

VI
Texas Strut

Oh George, thought Tony with great joy in his heart. *Pure ecstasy.*

Finally, he had managed to get away from his beloved wife Cherie and all the other *dead wood*, and was now in the company of the one true shining light of his life, George. He was feeling like the old Tony again, full of confidence, ready to take on the world, just like in the old days when entire continents had trembled with fear and awe at the merest mention of his name. Even the early rise at ten thirty hadn't bothered him too much because he was now sat next to George on a red tractor that was carrying the pair of them along a farm track on George's ranch.

George had appeared at breakfast after travelling overnight by private jet from Miami. The original idea had been for the two of them go out into the country to talk business but something had almost derailed these plans.

"You know Blair?" said George whilst driving, "Laura is really cut up about little Barney."

"Er, yes, right, it's a dreadful shame," said Tony, faking sympathy as best he could. "Do you know what caused his death?"

"No, but the vet's going to do a post-mortem."

Crumbs.

"What do you think made him go all wild like that, last night?" said George wiping away a tear.

"Er…"

"I mean, vomiting all over the house, attacking Mrs Blair like that and then just collapsing and dying. What's all that about? It just doesn't make any sense."

Gosh, thought Tony, burning up inside with fear, *if he starts to interrogate me, I know I'm going to crack.* "Who knows George, but erm, why did you invite me out here anyway?"

"I'm sorry Blair. Just give me a minute. I'm so cut up about that little *dawg*." George had wanted to cancel the meeting and was only here because Laura had insisted that he went ahead with it.

They drove on in silence but Tony didn't really mind. George was never the most communicative of people anyway and at least he had shut up about that awful *mutt*. Really, the only thing that mattered now was the question of the job that George was about to offer him and Tony was certain that it was going to be a good one.

George took a left-hand turn and stopped the tractor outside an old barn. He got down first and stood upright with his hands on his hips, gazing at the wooden structure.

As the Sun beat down strongly, Tony looked about and realised that they were probably the only people for miles around. He began to wonder if George really did know what had happened to Barney and had brought him out here to be killed in this isolated spot. *With cheese-wire or something horrible like that*, he thought looking around for assassins.

"Er, George…" he said climbing down from the tractor.

"You know Blair, when I was a little boy," said George now smiling, "my daddy hired fifteen Mexicans to build this old hog barn. Three of them died in the attempt."

"Er, yes, that's great George, but…"

"Those were the days. None of your PC crap then. You know Blair, when I was growing up, I was fascinated by all that NASA stuff and space. How about you?"

"Er, oh yes, George," said Tony, wondering where this was going. "I'm there every time the shuttle's on the telly."

"Well, just after my time as president was up, my Daddy got me a consultancy job working with those good old space boys down at NASA."

"Wonderful George, but…"

"Yeah isn't it? I'm now involved in fund-raising for NASA and trying to make space exploration more popular with the great American public."

"Fantastic George, but…"

"Well, for the last few months I've been taking part in some of the preliminary planning for a manned mission to the planet Mars."

That's very nice George, thought Tony impatiently, *but please can we start talking about my new job now.* The clouds began to clear in his head. He could see it now: Secretary General of the United Nations or maybe former president George Bush's personal envoy to the Gaza Strip. *Hell,* he would even settle to be George's new gardener or butler if that was what was offered.

George continued, "The mission's now about a year and a half from blast off and I'm helping to select the folks to go on the trip…"

Boring, thought Tony with his head still full of the top jobs he was about to pick from.

"…and in order to drum up enough public support and funds from Washington, I suggested to the HR boys down at NASA that we send a high-profile figure along on board to communicate the greatness of the mission to the people of the world."

Where is this leading? thought Tony feeling his dream job evaporating. "Er, what?"

"Yeah, and you know what Blair? I've put your name forward. You were first on my list."

"Er, that's great George but what did you *really* invite me out here for?" asked Tony taking his handkerchief from his pocket and wiping his brow.

"No Blair, this is it. I'm asking if you would like to go on the first manned mission to the planet Mars as my personal representative. What do you say buddy? Do you want to be one of the first men on Mars?"

"Er…" was all Tony could utter. The Texan Sun seemed hotter than ever now and his vision went blurry. He gripped the handkerchief and opened his mouth but no sound came out. *Gosh,* he thought feeling a strong rumble coming from his guts, *it's a good job this tracksuit's brown.*

VII

Sorry seems to be the Hardest Word

The tap dripped like the ticking of a clock.

The time was about six thirty in the evening and Tony was lying in the bath, trying to clean himself up after the *accident* at the hog barn earlier that day. His still-bandaged left foot was draped over the side of the tub as the doctor back in England had warned him to keep it dry for a few weeks. *Quacks*, he thought staring at the bubbles, *how many peace medals have they ever won?*

He closed his eyes and felt the boundaries between reality and the world of dreams start to blur. He could see his younger self running in his underpants under rain-filled clouds, being chased by nettle-wielding nuns across the school playing field and could still hear those evil witches cackle, *run Blair, run...* He shook his head and the memory slowly went to be replaced by more immediate worries. As he lay in the water, he tried to comprehend the proposal that George had made to him earlier at the barn. *Him*, Tony, going to another planet? Was it possible that he had somehow just misheard the offer?

George had already left the ranch and returned to Florida to personally convey the news of Tony's answer to NASA. Tony was beginning to wonder whether saying *yes* to George had really been the right answer.

George had said that the mission training would take at least eighteen months before blasting off in a rocket from Florida. The journey would take *ages* with about seven months spent on Mars followed by another long trip back to Earth. Tony and four other, as yet unnamed astronauts were to make up the crew. Officially, Tony was to be George's *special ambassador* and was to promote the mission before, during and after the trip to Mars.

Maybe, I could throw something electrical into the bath right now, he thought, looking around the bathroom. *Like a hairdryer or something. What about faking one's own death like that chap, Monkhouse who left his clothes on the beach?* He sighed with the realisation that when it came down to what was important, Tony felt that he just couldn't let George down after all this time, but how on Earth was he going to tell his beloved wife Cherie? *Oh George,* he thought dreamily, *I wish you were coming with me. Anyway*, he reasoned, the best way to tell her would be to just come straight out with it. *Look Cherie, I'm going to Mars. Just deal with it.*

Cherie was due to be discharged from the hospital at about six o-clock that evening after receiving treatment for dog bites. Tony had phoned her earlier to find out what her plans were but had said nothing about George's offer. Then he had spoken to her doctor who said that other than an awkward rabies injection, there were no complications from the attack, *alas*. Cherie was going to make a full recovery and she was probably on her way back to the ranch at this very moment.

Crumbs, he thought with the enormity of his decision dawning on him, *it doesn't matter what I say. She's going to go totally through the roof. I'll be eating those awful pies forever when I tell her what I've agreed to.*

If only he'd managed to get a proper job after leaving Downing Street. The talk from home was now all about *aggressive war* and other such nonsense. Perhaps, he really did have no option but to accept George's offer. It was indeed the best one he'd had in ages; in fact, it was the only one. Why, oh *why*, had he agreed to step aside for Gordon, *that double-crossing rat? I hope he's since died,* he thought remembering Gordon's downtrodden demeanour at the recent election loss.

From outside came the sound of a car pulling up on the drive. Tony leapt out of the bath and stood on the toilet seat. Looking out of the small ventilation window he could just about make out Cherie being helped out of the car.

Golly gosh, he thought desperately, *how the hell am I going to tell her?*

As his emotions raced, he tried stepping down from the toilet but instead slipped off the seat and fell into a tangled heap on the wet floor. Disappointed that he hadn't broken his neck or anything else, he crawled into the adjoining bedroom and lay on the bed.

Feelings of doom propelled him off the mattress and he began to get dressed into more of George's old togs. The trousers were a pair of gaudy red and white checked golfing slacks that were slightly tight. Tony checked to see if there were any more strange lumps in the pockets but found nothing but a stale digestive biscuit which he ate immediately and some typed notes about the Kennedy assassination marked *Secret*.

Boring, he thought binning the memo without reading it. Then he went to the wardrobe and from his jacket removed the old photo taken long ago of himself and George at this very ranch. *Oh George,* he thought staring in to George's all-knowing eyes, *blood, sugar, tears and sweat.* Suddenly, having to tell Cherie of his decision didn't seem quite so hard.

The Blairs' last evening in Texas was a sombre affair. At the dinner table sat Tony, his beloved wife Cherie and Barbara with Laura absent because of an upset stomach. Tony's rush of confidence in the bedroom had faded away almost completely now that he was about to *reveal all*.

"Are we not having more of my pies for dinner tonight, Barbara?" asked Cherie.

"Er, no Cherie dear," said Barbara hesitantly. "Chef was very insistent on cooking his speciality tonight."

Oblivious to the conversation, Tony stared blankly at the wall opposite, dissolutely stirring his soup with a spoon. Any lingering appetite for food had long since vanished. *What have I done?* he thought to himself despondently. *Mars?*

"You know Barbara," said Cherie, "I can get you a great deal on a hundred thousand of my pies."

"Erm, maybe later Cherie," said Barbara. "Anyway Tony, did you and George get your business out of the way?"

"Er, sorry?" said Tony still somewhat stupefied. "Oh yes, everything's fine."

"So, what happened then?" asked Cherie sharply.

"I'll tell you later dear. It's all very dull. I wouldn't want to bore our hostess."

"Oh no Tony," said Barbara, "I'd love to hear what George is up to. You know Cherie, that boy doesn't tell his mother anything. I usually only hear through his father."

"Er, where is old Mr Bush anyway," said Tony.

"Oh, he's at *CaliCryo* in San Diego at the moment," said Barbara. "He's volunteered for their latest research, but come on Tony…"

She's going to kill me, thought Tony miserably.

"…you must tell us what that no-good child of mine is up to now."

"Well, erm," he said desperately, "George sort of made me promise not to tell anyone yet as there are still quite a few details to iron out."

"Now Tony," said Barbara. "I'm George's mother. I know him better than he knows himself. He won't mind if you tell me of your plans."

This is it, thought Tony, seeing no way out. "Oh, it's no big deal really," he said sweating profusely with fear. "George just wants me to be his special ambassador that's all."

"Special ambassador?" said Cherie excitedly. "To where?"

"Er, just somewhere far away dear that's all," said Tony wiping his brow.

"Now Tony," said Barbara reprovingly, "your poor wife just wants to know where your next posting will be. It all sounds very exciting. Can't you just tell us a little bit about where you'll be going?"

"Erm, where I'm going," said Tony nervously, "it's a little bit chilly really and the air's a bit thin. That's all I can say at the moment."

"Well Cherie," said Barbara, "sounds like somewhere at altitude. Could it be Switzerland maybe?"

Gosh, thought Tony shaking his head, *I'm a dead man.* "Yes! That's it," he said quickly. "We're all off to Geneva to help George out."

"Well, that just great," said Barbara clapping once. "I'm so pleased for you folks."

Tony immediately regretted lying. "Erm, sorry did I say Geneva?" he whimpered. "I really meant to say, er, *Mars*."

"Mars where?" said Cherie. "What country is that in?"

"Er, no dearie, it's not in any country. It's the planet Mars."

"The planet Mars?" said Cherie incredulously.

"Yes, the planet Mars," repeated Tony.

"Is this some kind of a bad joke, Tony?" growled Cherie angrily.

"Er, George asked me this morning if I'd like to go to Mars and I said *yes*. I mean beggars can't be choosers, can they really dearie?"

"The planet *effin'* Mars!" raged Cherie. "Are you off your *bleedin'* rocker? I don't believe this. How could you, Tony?" With that she stood up, threw her napkin down and stormed out.

After a moment had passed, Barbara smiled awkwardly and said, "More wine Tony?"

"Er…" was all Tony could say, feeling his big toe really aching.

VIII
Careful with that Axe, Gordon

The cheering of the crowds was deafening as the ticker-tape rained down from above.

Tony smiled as he waved to the adoring multitudes from the back seat of a large open-top car that was being escorted by a police motorcade through the centre of Manhattan. He was heading for the United Nations Headquarters to make a speech about his latest triumph at the Middle East peace talks. All sides in the conflict had agreed to lay down their arms and live in peaceful coexistence thanks to his interventions. The Israelis and the Palestinians had finally agreed to put aside their differences. Insurgents in the Middle East had all promised to stop fighting. Even the Iranians had come round to giving up their nuclear weapons programme in a show of solidarity with his New World Order. And to top it all George was going to be there at the General Assembly building to present him with a peace medal. All that ridiculous talk of going to Mars and war crimes was now long forgotten, *thankfully*.

He turned to speak to his beloved wife Cherie seated next to him, but what he saw gave him an awful shock. Cherie had vanished and in her place, sat Gordon, grinning at him. "What are *you* doing here?" hissed Tony, "And what have you done with my wife?"

Gordon said nothing. He just kept smiling and waving.

"Hey fatty, I'm talking to you," said Tony as the car turned in to Dealey Plaza.

"Tony?" said a voice from the rear.

"Just a minute, George ..." he said turning to look behind as a bullet whizzed past close to where his head had just been.

"Tony?" The voice became louder, more insistent and the atmosphere darkened. Suddenly, the scene became all hazy and for a second everything went black.

"What?" said Tony groggily.

"Tony, wake up." It was his beloved wife Cherie, shaking him on the shoulder. "You were having a nightmare and shouting in your sleep."

"Eh? What was I saying?"

"Stuff like *you'll never get the top job*, *over my dead body* and *George, I love you*."

Crumbs, thought Tony despondently looking around the bedroom in *beautiful* Oxfordshire, *am I really still here in this dump?* Then the realisation of what he had recently agreed to, and that he was leaving for the United States in mere hours, hit him like a ton of bricks. But *yes,* it was all for George. *Oh George*, thought Tony adoringly, *to Hell and back*. At least Cherie had now accepted his decision to go to Mars. Possibly, the mission payment of one million dollars had helped to persuade her.

"What time is it?" asked Tony with a yawn.

"About three thirty," said Cherie.

"Oh no, I have to be up in eight hours."

"Look Tony, I've got an early start tomorrow as well. Carole is coming over before twelve with her new rectal endoscope. Do you want her to have good look around your insides when I'm done?"

"Er, no thanks dearie," said Tony pulling the duvet over his head. He shut his eyes firmly and tried to return to his ticker tape parade, hopefully *sans* Gordon. Instead, he was soon dreaming that he was waiting outside a court room on trial for war crimes. Two burly ushers appeared and dragged him inside.

Are you aware Mr Blair, asked the judge sternly, *as to the severity of your crimes?*

Erm, no, said Tony desperately. *I can't remember anything, honestly. It's all a complete mental block.*

How do you plead Mr Blair? demanded the judge.

Plead? Er, do I really have to enter a plea? I mean, I was only trying to help…

Mr Blair, said the judge donning a black cap, *I sentence you to death and a hundred pound fine. Take the prisoner away.*

No please, said Tony being dragged away towards the chopping block, *I was only following the advice.*

Gordon was there again, this time as executioner. He was still grinning as he stood next to the block, holding a giant axe. Tony awoke with a jump at the stroke of the blade on his neck to find his beloved wife Cherie snoring loudly next to him. The bedside clock told him it was now 5:42 a.m. and he felt like he'd had enough bad dreams for one night. So, he went downstairs, had some cheese from the fridge and phoned Texas again.

Later that morning, Tony was sat in the gym of his house shaking his wrist furiously. He wasn't exactly sure of the time as the second hand of his new wristwatch had stopped again. Apparently, the watch, a leaving gift from Jalal, was easily restarted with a quick shake of the wrist but that didn't seem to be the case now. Tony had been most impressed that someone on wages as low as Jalal's had been able to afford a Rolex.

Very shortly, Tony was leaving for London from where he was flying to the United States to begin the training for the recently-announced *Humans to Mars* Mission. Since returning to England from Texas, Tony's doubts about going to Mars had only increased. The trouble was there seemed to be so few other options available. Why, oh *why*, did George want him to go on such a dangerous mission anyway? He'd tried asking him but as usual George was never available to take any of his calls. According to George's mother, George was either out running, had a migraine or like yesterday, was at a funeral for a pet. *That bleedin' dog again!*

Tony tapped his fingers on the desk as he waited for Jalal to bring the car round to the front of the house. He noticed a discoloured patch of fresh plaster on the ceiling near the running machine where a large hole had been once been. *Shame about that hoop*, he thought nervously fingering the large purple rock crystal hanging around his neck that his beloved wife Cherie had left for him this morning. *Bleedin' claptrap*, he thought cynically as a car horn blew outside.

Slowly, he got to his feet, picked up the black suitcase lying next to the desk and walked to the door. He put one hand on the handle but just couldn't bring himself to open it. Memories from the past began to assail him. Why on Earth, had he stepped aside for that *Scottish traitor*? Just where were all of his old *so-called* friends with a top job and where, oh where was George? He turned around and looked at the telephone. *Life is just one long numbers game*, he thought philosophically. *George's number, the Chinese takeaway in the village, the Samaritans…*

His indecision vanished when all of a sudden, the phone rang. Maybe, this time it would be George with a reprieve for him! He dropped the case, ran to the desk and picked up the handset. "George?" he said into the mouthpiece.

"No, it's me," said his beloved wife Cherie, "did you get the extra strength karmic crystal I left on the kitchen table this morning?"

"Yes dearie," he said wearily, "I'm wearing it now."

"Well, make sure you keep wearing it. It'll help channel your positive spiritual energy and protect you from harmful nano-waves."

"I'm just about to go…"

"Carole's saying the probe has warmed up now so I'll have to go." *Clunk.*

Far too green and unpleasant, thought Tony slouched down on the back seat of a yellow car as the Oxfordshire countryside rolled past the window. Last week, without telling him, Cherie had traded the Bentley in for something called a *Prius*. According to Carole, the swap would do *wonders for their karma*. He winced at the prospect of being spotted by the press in such a *jalopy*.

"Remember Mr Tony," said Jalal from the front, "if they ask you anything, just say you were following the guidance of your advisors."

"Er..." said Tony, not feeling very conversational. Jalal was still Tony's official driver even though the Iraqi government was actively seeking his extradition for crimes against humanity. *What utter nonsense,* thought Tony who was only too keen for Jalal to remain in Britain as who knew whose head might be next in line on the block. *Bleedin' ingrates* he thought bitterly as the car turned on to the motorway.

To soothe his nerves, he removed the photo of himself with George in Texas from his jacket pocket and gazed at George's ruggedly handsome features once more. *Oh George,* he thought feeling his resolve stiffen, *no reverse gear.*

IX

A Dose of the Motel Blues

*B**leedin' watch*, thought Tony looking at his wrist. The *damned* thing had stopped again. He shook his hand and reset the time to 18:58 from a digital clock on the wall opposite him in the conference room. He made a mental note to get Jalal to write to Rolex and complain about their *shoddy* workmanship when he got back to England. *When was that again?*

"Ladies and gentlemen, members of the press," said the grey-haired man sitting next to him in the uniform of the United States Navy. "Welcome to Miami and the Beach Hilton Hotel for the beginning of an incredible voyage: *Humans to Mars*. My name is Rear Admiral Lesley Sayers and I'm in charge of this media debrief tonight on behalf of NASA. Tonight, is mainly about introductions to the crew as you guys have already received an outline of the mission itinerary. First of all,

I'll introduce the key personnel and then we'll take a few questions.

"You guys ready now?" said Sayers looking left and right at the five men and one woman sat with him. Not seeing any dissent, he turned to face the waiting crowd of journalists. "Well, ladies first and on my left is Dr Alice Siberry. Among her many distinctions, Dr Siberry was the first woman to fly combat jets with the US Air Force. On the mission to Mars she will be in charge of medical matters and will hold the rank of Colonel."

A thin grey-haired woman with pigtails waved to the audience.

"Next to Alice, we have former prime minister Tony Blair from Great Britain. Tony's role is to be former president George W Bush's special ambassador to the *Humans to Mars* Mission. Tony's going to be communicating to you guys and the wider public the good news about the mission and its affiliated sponsors."

Journalists, thought Tony bitterly, *how many elections have they ever won?* "Er, yeah, great to be here everyone," he said waving his arm.

"On my right is the mission commander," said Sayers indicating the man with a thatch of white hair sat next to Siberry, "Colonel James Collins. Colonel Collins served with the United States Air Force in the Korean and Vietnam wars and was decorated in both of those conflicts."

Collins smiled confidently and acknowledged the crowd of journalists.

"Sitting next to Commander Collins is Colonel Leonard Stewart, the mission's second-in-command

and an old combat buddy of mine. Colonel Stewart was the youngest pilot to fly with the United States Navy in Vietnam and has since worked tirelessly to improve the welfare of naval veterans."

Stewart, another white-haired man with a neat moustache gave a wave.

Sayers went on, "On Colonel Stewart's right is Chief Engineer Robert Marshall. Chief Marshall is the mission's scientific officer and is a damned fine engineer to boot. Originally from Honolulu, Chief Marshall began his career on the Manhattan Project and later designed the oxygen tanks for the Apollo 13 mission."

Marshall who was completely bald raised his hand.

"And lastly but certainly not least, next to Tony Blair is the overall mission supremo, Brian Wallace. I've known Brian for twenty years at NASA and I can't imagine this undertaking being in any finer hands. Brian will be taking care of the astronauts all the way from initial training to co-ordinating their stay on Mars from Earth and back home again."

A stern-looking bald man with a ruddy complexion stared unsmilingly back at the crowd of journalists.

"Okay," said Sayers rubbing his hands, "detailed bios are available from NASA online people, so I'm not going to bore you any longer with minutiae about this fine crew. Now, we'll take questions from the floor, er… you sir," said Sayers pointing to a man at the front.

"Mr Blair, Martin Becker, ABC News," said the journalist. "Just why has former President Bush asked you to go along on what is essentially a very dangerous mission at the extremes of scientific and technological knowledge?"

Dangerous? "Oh, come now Martin," said Tony feeling his big toe starting to ache, "I think we all know that NASA has an excellent track record in these areas and that if anyone can succeed in getting us to Mars and back, it is them."

"Excellent track record?" said Becker. "What about the *Challenger* accident?"

"Accident?" said Tony shaking his head. "Sorry, but I'm not following you."

"The *Challenger* disaster, January 28th 1986?"

"Nope sorry, you've still lost me."

"The shuttle *Challenger* blew up in mid-air in 1986 with the loss of all seven crew on board."

"What?" said Tony incredulously. "You mean one of these *bleedin'* planes has already crashed?"

"Not just one, Mr Blair," replied Becker, "the shuttle *Columbia* was also destroyed when it disintegrated during re-entry into Earth's atmosphere in 2003, again with the loss of all on board."

"Er, I'm sure NASA will make it work," said Tony unconvincingly.

"Can I refer you back to my original question please, Mr Blair," continued Becker. "Why do you think you were selected to go on the mission?"

Sayers interrupted, "I will field this one if you don't mind, Tony."

"Er, no Admiral," said a relieved Tony, "go ahead,"

Sayers glowered at the audience, "Former President George W Bush spoke to me just before I left for Miami and he said that he needed a solid and reliable anchor on this mission between himself, the crew and the folks back on Earth. There is no better communicator than former prime minister Tony Blair. Next question please, you sir."

"Henry Owens, *Chicago Tribune*," said a besuited bald man three rows back. "Mr Blair, do you think that at your age and given your medical history, you will be up to the huge challenge of a mission to Mars?"

You cheeky… "Well," said Tony, now feeling very hot, "I've been keeping myself in good shape down at my home gym since I retired from politics and my GP's given me a clean bill of health so I can't really foresee a problem there."

Owens persisted, "But Mr Blair, this is an incredibly hazardous mission that will take almost three years to complete. Are you sure that a man with a heart condition like yours should be going on such a long and difficult voyage?"

"Now look here," insisted Tony sounding flustered, "I've told you already that I'm in tip top health. I'm sure that the medical chaps at NASA will make sure that we are all trained to the peak of physical fitness. Next question please." He took a handkerchief from his pocket and wiped the moisture from his brow. He could feel his heart beating really fast. Who on Earth were these people, thinking they could give him, *Tony*, such a hard time?

"You're popular tonight, Tony," said Sayers smiling at him then turning to a brown-haired woman in the second row, "you madam."

"Simone Lowe, CNN," said the woman. "Mr Blair, is this trip to Mars not just a distraction from the fact that you are likely to face charges at a war crimes tribunal in the near future?"

Why can't these people just leave me alone? "Oh, come now Simone," said Tony as breezily as he could, "I think we all know that nothing is going to come of any of that. I stand by my conviction that it was in the national interest of the United Kingdom to intervene in Iraq alongside the United States. I am sure the courts and History itself, will judge me on that. Next question please."

"I'm sorry Mr Blair," said Lowe, "but do you not feel that this mission to Mars is just some kind of get-out clause?"

"Er..." said Tony certain that his big toe was hurting more than ever.

"Excuse me Tony," said Sayers interrupting again, "but I'll take this one. You see *Miz* Lowe, little people like yourself, cannot see the bigger picture. What you have here in front of you, is a great man doing great deeds; deeds that mere mortals like yourself can only dream about. There are very big things afoot here and all you can do is harp on about the little things. The war finished a long time ago, my friend. It's ancient history, it's done and, ladies and gentlemen, so is this press conference. I bid you all goodnight." With that Sayers stood up and after patting each crew member on the back, left for his aircraft carrier.

Later in the hotel bar, Tony spotted Arnold Schwarzenegger talking with a young blonde woman. "How was I, Arnie?" said Tony, inserting himself into the conversation.

Schwarzenegger looked puzzled.

"You know," said Tony, "the press conference. You did see it?"

"Oh Tony darling," said Schwarzenegger flatly, "you were fantastic."

"I knew it," said Tony excitedly, "I still haven't lost the old magic, you know."

"Sorry Tony, but I must now go," said Schwarzenegger draining his glass, "I am filming a new movie."

"Oh, great. What's it about?"

"It is called *Iraq: The Movie*. I play the President and Kevin Spacey is Saddam Hussein. It is an action musical."

"Oh well, I can sing a bit you know, if you've got any spare roles floating about."

"Sorry Tony, but the entire movie has been cast."

"Oh well, if anyone drops out… I've got an agent now, you know."

"Yes Tony," said Schwarzenegger, putting his jacket on "Come on baby, let's go. I'll be in touch, Tony."

"Er, when can I expect to hear from you?"

"I'll call you," said Schwarzenegger who then left with his blonde friend.

The bar was empty of customers now except for Tony. Before he could leave, a barman walked over and said, "Hey buddy, ain't you that Brown fellow from England?"

What?! thought Tony angrily. "Blair," he said icily, "Tony Blair."

"Nice to meet you," said the barman offering his hand. "I'm sorry about that name thing. The old memory's still a little shaky. I've still got some grenade fragments stuck up here." The man smiled and pointed to a scar on his crown.

"Think nothing of it," said Tony limply accepting the gesture.

"My name's Geoff. Will you have a drink with me? Eight years in the US Marine Corps and three tours of Iraq and Afghanistan."

I don't drink with peasants. "Er, no thanks," said Tony scurrying for the exit.

X
Making Plans for Tony

The air conditioner made a low whirring sound.
"Wake up, Blair," said a distant voice.

Slowly, Tony opened his eyes and yawned. He blinked and realised a bald red-faced man was staring angrily at him from the front of the room.

"I was just erm…" said Tony groggily.

"This is the final mission debrief and you can't even stay awake for it," said Brian Wallace perspiring heavily. "You're leaving tomorrow, Blair. For Mars."

"Er…" was all Tony could say as he was feeling absolutely terrible. *Has it really come down to this?* he thought incredulously. *Mars?!* He still couldn't believe that he was really going. *Tomorrow?* This whole thing felt like some kind of bad dream and it seemed possible that any moment he could wake up from this nightmare. *If only…* If only he'd managed to get a proper job instead of this *fiasco*. It also didn't help that he'd had to get up at ten thirty this morning.

He was sat on a chair in the pre-launch meeting room at the Kennedy Space Centre in Florida. Sitting on the same row of seats, were his fellow *Humans to Mars* crewmates, all of whom were rather old. Apparently, Stewart was in his late seventies, both Collins and Siberry were eighty-something and Marshall had just hit ninety. Tony had tried to ask George why he was going on such a dangerous mission with *a load of old biddies* but as usual George was unavailable. Cheeseborough, George's butler had proffered the opinion that life experience was essential to the success of the mission and that "these were the best guys available".

"Now that we're all awake," said Wallace looking at Tony again. "I'm sure you've all heard this before but I'm gonna say it anyway: tomorrow afternoon, ladies and gents at 1pm Eastern Standard Time, the *Blue Bull* will carry you all into low Earth orbit…" He clicked on the mouse and a picture of a rocket came up on the big screen.

Boring, thought Tony feeling his eyelids becoming very heavy again as Wallace began to *rattle* on about the mission.

"…with the journey to Mars taking about 280 days." The image of a space craft orbiting the Earth came on the screen. "After tomorrow's launch your first port of call is the International Space Station currently orbiting four hundred clicks above the Earth. Waiting there for you now is the fully-provisioned orbiter, the *USS McDonald* which will take you all the way to Mars and back again. Any questions so far?"

Tony raised his hand, "Can I go to the toilet please?"

"No, you cannot," said Wallace firmly. "You'll have to wait until the end of the meeting. You know something, Blair, this is not just a walk down to your club. Mars is 500 million kilometres away. It's going to be *real* tough."

"Er, sorry Brian," said Tony meekly. Ever since meeting Wallace at the Miami Beach Hilton almost two years ago, Tony had felt a lack of *chemistry* between himself and the mission head. Wallace's belief in Tony's complete unsuitability for a journey to Mars had been aired many times during the training period. *Thank goodness*, George had never lost faith in him.

"Fantastic," said Wallace, wiping his brow with a paper tissue. "Next, on reaching Mars, you're going to spend almost eight months down on the surface. Remember, Tony to keep those adverts coming otherwise the mission budget could fall short…"

Tony smiled weakly. *Whenever my haemorrhoids cause me discomfort, I turn to the soothing pain relief of new Anusoft, the official haemorrhoid cream of the Humans to Mars Mission.*

"…then it's another nine months in the orbiter back to Earth. So, if all goes to plan," Wallace looked at Tony again, "that's about twenty six months until you return."

Oh George, thought Tony sleepily, *one minute without you is too long.*

After pausing for effect Wallace continued, "Martian days are only about forty minutes longer than those on Earth but the seasons are about twice as long. Because it's further from the Sun than Earth, Mars is cold, *very* cold.

Even though you're going to be setting up base camp near the Martian equator, you'll be lucky most days if the temperature breaks freezing point. Typically, you're looking at a maximum of about thirty Fahrenheit down to about minus two twenty in the daytime. Things can get real extreme out there, especially at night, so watch out."

...ladies and gentlemen of the Academy, said Tony, holding a golden statuette, *I'd like to dedicate my award to...*

"The atmosphere of Mars is much thinner than Earth's at about seven millibars and it's toxic, roughly 95% C-O-two. So, if you venture out of the base, you're going to need a suit and a respirator. No suit means all bodily fluids boil away in minutes." Wallace paused again to look at a fast-asleep Tony, "Wake up Tony. This information might just save your life."

Tony opened his eyes and began rubbing his face, "What, oh erm, I just had something in my eye, honest."

Wallace sighed and continued, "This next bit's really important. You're taking a number of oxygen cylinders with you to Mars. The respirators can be replenished from the cylinders, but you've got to remember to make sure that any used respirators have been purged of any remaining gases before being refilled. If this doesn't happen, the gauges can say the respirator is full of air when in reality it might be nearly empty. Bob, as science officer, you're in charge of that one."

Scientists, thought Tony dismissively, *how many elections have they ever won?*

"Next," Wallace continued, "Mars is invariably windy and that means dust is a going to be a problem. This stuff is extremely fine and abrasive. On the Moon the space suits were leaking after two days because of small particulates. It'll be like that on Mars but worse. If you go outside, you've got to really dust yourselves off when you get back in the air-lock. Work in pairs and check each other out for holes; make sure the other guy or gal is dust-free using the soft brushes in the air-lock. The air filtration system will then take care of the rest. Any rips in the suits have got to be dealt with immediately or you could find yourselves out there without any air. Did you get any of that Tony?"

"Er, check," said Tony blinking to try and stay awake.

Wallace stared at him as he clicked on the mouse to reveal a close-up image of a barren, rubble-strewn panorama. "This is NH 561719, the hundred or so metre square zone on which the Mars base will be sited. The area was chosen for its relative flatness but that doesn't make it smooth enough for the orbiter to land on." *Click.* The image of a small shuttle-like craft appeared on the screen. "To overcome this difficulty, our engineers have developed a reusable transporter, known as the *USS Heinz,* to ensure the safe transfer of crew and equipment down to the surface of Mars. You're taking it to Mars on the underbelly of the *McDonald.* The *Heinz* can carry two astronauts and a small payload of equipment down to the surface at a time, allowing the *McDonald* to stay in orbit around Mars, a far less risky proposition than trying to land it on the surface.

"Piloting duties are restricted to Collins, Siberry and Stewart. That's about it, people. Does anyone have any questions?"

"Have you got the right time, Brian?" said Tony shaking his wrist. "This *bleedin'* watch keeps stopping."

Wallace went even redder, "Will you please stop veering away from the subject under discussion with your irrelevant requests and petty questions, Blair."

I only asked, thought Tony indignantly. "Sorry again," he simpered.

"It's twelve forty, Tony," said a smiling Chief Marshall sat next to him.

"It's a Rolex, you know," said Tony showing his wrist to Marshall.

"Any serious final points, people?" asked Wallace wearily. This time nobody spoke. "Right then, Commander Collins is going to say a few words now about the living arrangements on your journey and on the base. James please."

"Thanks Chief," said Collins stepping out to the front. He clicked on the mouse and a blueprint of the orbiter came up on the screen. "This is the plan of the *McDonald*, people. It's modelled on the *Challenger* design but with modifications for crossing deep space such as extra radiation shielding."

Radiation? thought Tony fearfully.

"Each astronaut had been assigned a small cabin on the lower deck," continued Collins. "Tony and Robert, you're on this side whilst Alice and Leonard, you're on the opposite wall. Being mission commander, I get a separate bunk in a narrow space next to the payload bay." *Click*. The plan of a building appeared on the screen. "Our home on Mars, known officially as *Barclays* Mars Base Alpha is built using aluminium poles and an impermeable canvas in order to keep out the Martian atmosphere, and to provide insulation from the low temperatures and extreme dryness on the surface of Mars."

All that way to sleep in a bleedin' tent, thought Tony blearily.

"There are three main parts to the base," said Collins pointing a metre stick at the screen. "Firstly, this circular central section is the biome, which is basically a giant greenhouse made from transparent plastic panels to allow the Martian sunlight to penetrate inside so we can grow plants for food and oxygen. Alice, you're in charge of this area. These smaller circles leading off, are the sleeping and meeting areas. Again, the sleeping arrangements are similar to those on the *McDonald.*" *Click.* The image of a tall cuboidal metallic structure appeared on the screen. "The mission's water requirements are going to come from a large deposit of ice identified by Mars probes that lies about a metre under the base. In order to get at this, special drilling equipment is being brought from Earth. Tony, you've had extensive training on the rig so this one's your department. Tony?"

Tony didn't answer …*senators, congressmen, members of the jury, boys and girls, I'd like to dedicate this Presidential Freedom Medal to…*

"Tony?" repeated Collins.

"Oh absolutely," said Tony somewhat glassy-eyed.

"I was just saying that you've had training on the drilling rig"

The worst ever time of my life. "Er, check." Tony

had spent a month in Texas reluctantly learning about *automated drilling systems.* Strangely, George had been too busy to visit him even though the drilling centre was located in Crawford.

"Okay Chief," said Collins, "that's it from me."

"Right, people," said Wallace returning to the front, "last thing from me: stick together, believe in one another and some of you might just stay alive down there long enough to get back home. Anyone want to say anything before we finish?"

Tony blinked and raised his arm.

"Yes Tony?" said a tired-sounding Wallace.

"Erm, just if you've got anyone else on stand-by who's really disappointed on missing out going to Mars then you know, I'd be more than willing to, er, step aside."

"Sorry Tony," said Wallace, "but such an individual does not exist."

"I thought I'd mention it just in case," said Tony. "Er, I am looking forward to going really."

"If only that were true," said Wallace sighing heavily. "So people, tomorrow is no dress rehearsal. I want everyone to get plenty of rest tonight because you're going to need it." Wallace looked at Tony once more. "Don't forget to say your last goodbyes and for some of you that might just be the truth."

Oh George, thought Tony despairingly, *what is truth?*

XI
The Nightmare before Lift-off

Local time was five minutes to one in the afternoon at Cape Canaveral Air Force Station in Florida. A crowd of space enthusiasts, crew family members, journalists and NASA personnel had gathered in the observation gantry at the Kennedy Space Centre to watch the imminent blast-off. In the distance a giant space rocket, standing proudly upright, could be seen with the words *Blue Bull* written down the side. On top of the rocket was the Command Module, *Walmart* in which a crew of five astronauts lay awaiting lift-off.

Bleedin' giant firework, thought Tony gripping tightly on the grab-handles at his side. The countdown clock in the narrow space above his head was fixed on sixty seconds. He shut his eyes and tried not to think about the desperate situation he now found himself in, but that was harder said than done. *Why oh why oh why oh why*, had he agreed to step down as prime minister for that *Scottish splitter* and why was George still not returning his calls? Last night, he had phoned George's ranch in Texas but yet again had only managed to speak to George's mother, who told him that George had gone out night-fishing and had turned his mobile phone off. Barbara had reassured him though that George would be watching the launch tomorrow and would be "rooting for him". Tony had been really disappointed not to be able to speak to George again as he had wanted to pitch to him a new reality-TV show he had thought up called *Guantanamo Bay or Bust*, whereby members of the public or even better, famous people (*Celebrity Guantanamo*) would be imprisoned in the military prison at Guantanamo Bay and would try to win their freedom by performing zany tasks on camera.

…come on Mr Barrowman, into the dog cage now…

After phoning Texas, Tony had said goodbye to Cherie and the kids at their hotel and then after struggling to come up with another contact, phoned Mr Ho, his gardener back home in Oxfordshire. Mr Ho had said that it was three o-clock in the morning there and as he had to be up early to go down to the cash-and-carry for gardening supplies, he couldn't really speak for long. He then mentioned that the police had been nosing around the village asking questions about a bomb at which Tony had laughed weakly and then hung up immediately.

As he waited for blast-off, memories of the mission training came back to him like the last thoughts of a condemned man waiting on the scaffold. The first six months had been spent in Florida learning to fly. Tony fondly recalled his flight instructor proudly boasting that he had trained two of the 9/11 pilots to fly commercial airliners, but was a bit *put out* that his final flight report recommended he never flew solo. *Tendency to day-dream, my...* Thank *heavens* George had never lost faith in his abilities.

Following that, months were spent in an enormous swimming pool practicing weightlessness drills after which Tony had joked on endlessly to anyone who would care to listen, that his feet had grown webbing. Then there had been the endless lectures: completely tedious, jargon-heavy *sermons* which he found generally incomprehensible. *Boffins,* thought Tony, *how many elections have they ever won?*

Near the end of the training programme, Tony had spent three months living in a tent on a wind-swept barren rock called Surtsey in order to acclimatise to conditions that were thought to be similar on the surface of Mars. Tony had found this experience to be particularly horrible as Surtsey truly was a God-forsaken wilderness where it was impossible to get a phone signal and nothing grew except mould. *Oh George*, thought Tony wistfully, *islands in the stream.*

The final part of the training had been a month spent in Hollywood learning how to make advertising videos for the seemingly-endless list of mission sponsors. He found it all a bit demeaning that he, *Tony*, once such a pre-eminent world statesman was now publicly endorsing the great new cleaning powers of *ToiletFresh*, the official lavatory cleaning product of the *Humans to Mars* Mission and such like. At least George's mother had said that George would get him a proper job when he got back from Mars. *Just when was that again?* Barbara hadn't actually specified which particular job but it was bound to be a good one. In reality, Tony didn't care really what it was, even cleaner or handyman as long as he was able to work with George again. *Oh George,* he thought dreamily, *why couldn't you be going as well?*

If only another role had come up instead of this terrible one. At least all that ridiculous talk about war crimes should have died down by the time he got back to Earth. Last month, some chap at the UN had even suggested that he, *Tony*, should stand trial at the International Court of Justice in The Hague for waging aggressive war. *Holland,* he thought bitterly, *how many wars have they ever won?*

He reflected that this could be the last day he would ever spend on Earth which in some ways was a good thing given how unpopular he still seemed to be. At least, the *proles* seemed to be more interested in him now judging by the hundreds of letters and emails he was receiving from around the world. George had even provided his *special ambassador* with a secretary to open them all and reply on his behalf. *Good old George,* he thought warmly, *always thinking of others*. Apparently, one of the letters had even been positive and friendly towards him.

Just then he felt something moving about in his trouser pocket. At first, he couldn't figure out what it was but then realised that it was his mobile phone ringing. *Technically*, he wasn't supposed to have his phone so close to the instrumentation but he was willing to take the risk in case George rang. Quickly, he worked the phone out of his flight suit and looked at the caller name. It was a withheld number but he was sure he knew who was calling. *Oh George*, thought Tony ecstatically, *I knew you wouldn't let me down.* He pressed the answer button and said "George?"

"Tony, it's Selwyn, your agent. How's things?"

"Er…" said Tony somewhat crestfallen that yet again, it wasn't George.

"Anyway," said the agent, "I hope you've finished that book by now because I've got some good news for you. A little bird at Channel 5 is telling me that *The Shining* is going ahead and the producers think that you would be great for the part of Grady the bartender. Can you get down here in the morning?"

Rats! "Er, sorry old chap but I'm afraid I'm going to be tied up for a bit. Can you try and stall them while I'm away?"

Outside, the main booster rockets began warming up and the noise inside the command module became deafening.

"Sorry," said Tony, having to raise his voice. "What was that?" He looked at his phone and saw the signal had been lost.

"Mission control, do you copy?" said Commander Collins lying next to Tony. "This bird is ready to fly. Repeat, this bird is ready to fly."

Ready to die more likely, thought Tony, gripping ever more tightly onto the grab-handles. *Mars? Was this really my only option?*

"One minute," said a voice from the tannoy. The countdown clock began its task.

Am I really going to another planet?

When the clock reached the final ten seconds a woman's voice filled the command module, "Ten, nine, eight…"

How did it ever come to this? thought Tony, more terrified than ever before of what lay in front of him.

"…seven, six, five…"

Oh George, he thought feverishly, *why aren't you here with me?*

"…four, three, two…"

Crumbs!

"…one."

"GEORGE!!!" screamed Tony as the rocket he was sitting on, fired powerfully into life. For a microsecond nothing happened then slowly the rocket began to move, mere inches at first but then much faster. Through a small porthole Tony could see the Earth fall away and strong forces assailed his hold on consciousness. *Oh dear,* he thought queasily as blue gave way to black, *I hope I packed some clean underpants.*

Time seemed to stand still in Texas as the Sun beat down through a cloudless azure sky.

"What's that, Blair?" said George from his perch on a stool at the side of a small lake.

"I said," said Tony removing from his head the hat he'd found in the wardrobe this morning, "absolutely any…"

"Who's that coming our way?" said George pointing to a figure crossing the bridge leading from the main house.

On time for once. "It's only, er…" said Tony hesitantly.

"Oh, and you know something else, Blair," said George turning round to face him.

"Yes George?" he said staring into George's steely blue eyes, knowing at this very moment George was about to tell him that he loved him. How could his life ever get any better than right now? *Oh George*, he thought adoringly, *flying without wings…*

--- End of Part 1 ---

Life on Mars

Mars has an atmosphere consisting of mainly carbon dioxide (95% CO_2, 3% nitrogen, 2% argon) and has the three forms of water. It is much smaller than Earth (6 794 km diameter to 12 742 km).

Mars has about one third of Earth's gravitational force at the surface but only one tenth of its mass.

The Martian atmosphere is more than one hundred times thinner than Earth's.

Mars is red because of iron oxide in the surface material possibly from iron reacting with free oxygen in the early atmosphere.

Mars can experience planet-wide dust storms and is generally very arid. Wispy clouds (probably from the sublimation of ice) are common.

It is thought that most of the original Martian water was

lost about 3 billion years ago. The effects of water channels from those early times are still evident on the surface of Mars today.

The Martian axis tilts at 25.2° so Mars shows seasonality at least as much as Earth (23.5°) does. Martian seasons are much longer than those on Earth because a year on Mars lasts 687 Earth days.

The Martian surface receives dangerously high levels of radiation even though it is further from the Sun than Earth because of a weak magnetosphere*.

A weak magnetosphere indicates that the interior of Mars is less dynamic than the Earth's mantle and core. Mars has been more geologically active in the past judging by its (now mostly-extinct) volcanoes.

The possible evolution of life from chemical means may have occurred independently of that on Earth. The focus on any manned Martian expeditions would be this.

Voyagers to Mars would suffer mentally and physically from the privations of loneliness and containment so the recruitment of older, more resilient astronauts is seen as advantageous.

The astronauts would be expected to man a Mars base

---

* The space around Mars affected by its magnetic field.

until relieved by the next Mars crew. The expectation that initial crews will return to Earth is low.

Solar radiation and collisions with rocky debris between Earth and Mars would be amongst the main hazards on the journey.

Using a gravitational sling-shot escape from Moon or Earth would increase the momentum of any space craft. The journey to Mars is considered to take at least seven months.

It is thought that oxygen could be extracted from CO_2 whilst plants could be co-opted to grow hydroponically. The surface of Mars could contain amounts of hydrogen peroxide which is a ready store of oxygen.

Ultimately, some scientists think that Mars could be made hospitable to humans (terraformed).

Part Two

Tony on Mars

I

Into the Void

Tony was jamming with Jimi Hendrix backstage. Hendrix had asked Tony to show him a few licks on the guitar after the concert had finished.

"Look here," said Tony pointing at the fretboard, "you put your fingers here…"

"Oh Tony," said Hendrix, "you're the greatest."

"Well, you know…" said Tony trying to sound modest.

"Do you want to hear my new song?" asked Hendrix. "It goes a bit like this …"

Tony was deeply unimpressed as the song was nothing but a series of electronic bleeps. Just then everything started to blur and he realised that he wasn't back in England with Jimi Hendrix but instead was lying in his quarters inside a ridiculous *tin box* known as the *USS McDonald*. The 9am 'morning' alarm had just sounded to impose some discipline on a realm that acknowledged no time frame. *Especially when one's watch kept stopping,* thought Tony shaking his wrist vigorously.

Just where was he going again? *Mars?* He lay back on his pillow and felt a dark mood take hold. Why hadn't he listened to all the naysayers and doubters back home when he'd had the chance? And now at George's behest, he was hurtling towards an unfeasibly distant rock known as *bleedin'* Mars. Just why had George sent him on such a dangerous mission in the first place? He was starting to find it all a bit odd as his duties on board were so minimal; there really didn't seem that much point in him being there. All he really had to do, apart from attending meals and meetings, was make the occasional video for the myriad of mission sponsors. *Give your loved ones peace of mind with Irish Provident, the official funeral plan insurance providers of the Humans to Mars Mission.*

To relieve his depression, he gazed at a photograph that he'd pressed into a gap in the panelling near his head. It was the image of himself with George taken at George's ranch in Texas all those years ago. He stared into George's serenely beautiful eyes and felt all his recent tribulations dissolve into nothingness. Once more, he knew deep down that there was no greater love. *Oh George*, he thought giving the image a gentle pat, *your reasons are your own.*

George's reassuring gaze though didn't solve the problem of what to do next. How *the blazes* was he going to fill his time in until they arrived on Mars? *The old memoirs?* He'd managed to come up with the title, *One Man's Journey* but that was it so far. He firmly believed that an autobiography was something one got someone else to write when one's career was actually over and he was determined that his wasn't. *The diary?* Before leaving Earth, *The Daily Mail* had agreed to pay him a hundred thousand pounds upfront for his day-by-day account of the mission. So, with a deep sigh he took a pen and notepad from under his bunk and manoeuvred himself onto his front in order to write.

Dear diary we blasted off last week from Florida and spent two days at the ISS...

Tony hadn't thought much of the International Space Station. He was expecting something like in that film *2001: A Space Odyssey*, but instead, had found the station to be rather makeshift, cramped and very smelly. In charge of the ISS and its sole occupant was a Russian named Boris Zhirkhov. Commander Zhirkov had been on board the ISS for over a thousand days already, mostly on his own as part of an experiment into the effects of solitude in space on the human body and mind. Zhirkov had been very pleased to see them but Tony had been a bit shocked by his wild grey hair, long straggly beard and the loincloth made from the remnants of his flight suit. To make matters worse, he had called Tony an *imperialist pig* and said that he much preferred Gordon to him. *Bleedin' foreigners,* thought Tony bitterly, *always stealing your job.*

For Tony, the final proof of Zhirkov's insanity was when he declared his undying affection for Tony's beloved wife Cherie. *A complete fruitloop,* he thought trying to erase from his memory the image of a semi-naked cosmonaut waving wildly at them through a porthole whilst clutching a photograph of Mrs Blair. *Spacemen*, thought Tony, *how many political parties have they ever led?*

He sighed, put the diary away and then to cheer himself up opened his email account as it had been hours since he'd last checked his inbox. He found he had nearly a hundred new messages mostly from space enthusiasts enquiring about how the journey to Mars was progressing. The remainder were from families of soldiers killed in Iraq and Afghanistan. Just who were these *peasants,* he thought with a forceful stab of the delete button, thinking that they could harangue him, *Tony* whenever they felt like it? His indignation vanished though when, to his great joy he realised there was actually an email from George.

George has received your email and values it highly. Unfortunately, he is extremely busy right now and will reply when he can.

Disappointingly, the email said nothing about what George thought about his idea for a new talent show for the pets of celebrities to be called *Sausages* but at least it showed that George was still there for him. He stared again at the Polaroid above his pillow and knew that the bond between them was stronger than ever now that he was working for George as his special ambassador. *Oh George,* thought Tony looking out into the blackness of space through a porthole near his head, *tender is the night…*

Just then a bleeping sound filled his cabin and the visage of Commander Collins appeared on the video screen near his pillow.

"Morning Tony," said Collins smiling at him, "we've

got an important transmission from NASA incoming for all ears so can you come on down to the bridge please."

"What now?"

"Sure thing."

"Oh, I'd love to but I've got these important, er, letters to, erm…"

"Are you sure Tony? I think former President Bush is going to speak."

"I'm on my way now," said Tony leaping from his bunk.

In the cockpit, Tony found his fellow crew members strapped in to their flight seats. Tony was extremely suspicious of all four of them because they were all very old and far too nice.

"Hey Tony," said Colonel Siberry winking at him as he strapped himself in, "I'm just restarting the mainframe and then we should receive the transmission.

"Delta, Foxtrot, Tango. *Humans to Mars* Mission here," said Siberry. "Repeat, Delta, Foxtrot, Tango. *Humans to Mars* mission here. Earth, what is your status?" She paused. "Just about there, I think we've got visuals… now."

Tony's heart leapt as the monitor above the cockpit windows flickered into life. An image of Old Glory filled the screen and the *Star-Spangled Banner* played from the command console speakers. Then the face of a grey-haired man flickered on to the screen in front of a large NASA logo. "Hey Mars crew!" chimed George, "How y'all doing up there?"

Oh George, thought Tony ecstatically, *hallowed be thy name.*

"Thank you, Mr President, everyone's fine here," said Commander Collins.

"I'd just like to congratulate you all on your progress over the last few weeks," said George with a smile. "Only another two hundred or so days to go until you reach your destination."

Oh George, thought Tony despairingly, *one day without you is too long.*

"We will endure, Mr President," said Collins steadfastly. "We will endure."

"Commander Collins," said George, "do you have a message for the people of the world?"

Crumbs, thought Tony nervously, feeling his big toe starting to hurt, *I hope he's not expecting me to speak.*

"Just that we're trying to expand the frontiers of science and knowledge up here," said Collins, "in order to make life much better for the folks down there on Earth."

"Well, that's just great," replied George. "Is Blair there?"

Tony heart skipped a beat and he raised his hand. "I'm here George," he squeaked nervously.

"Yo Blair, how are you doing buddy? You'll never guess the fantastic surprise we've arranged for you up there."

Oh George, thought Tony, almost fainting at George's kind words, *I knew you wouldn't let me down.*

"You know those pies that Mrs Blair brought over to the house before your mission training began?" asked George.

"Er, yes George?" said Tony.

"Well, great news. We've had one of them analysed by

the good old boys down here at NASA and it seems that they're the perfect food for your trip to Mars."

What?! thought Tony starting to smell a rat.

"Yeah buddy," George continued, "I've got the piece of paper from the lab here in front of me now. The pastry is made from a highly durable mixture of flour, newspaper and industrial disinfectant making it incredibly resistant to decay. The actual meat of the pie took the lab guys quite a time to pin down, but we think it's about 20% rodent and 30% canine, with the rest being sawdust, clay and water. It's also extremely low in cholesterol making it ideal as a healthy and nutritious protein source. Well…"

Oh no, thought Tony, feeling his imminent recall evaporating, *where is this going?*

"…as a special surprise the boys who packed the *McDonald*, included a few of those pies in their deliveries and…"

A few?

"…in the payload bay there is a whole section full of Mrs Blair's pies."

"Full?" said Tony.

"Yeah Blair, just over ten thousand delicious pastries," said George breaking into a smile. "That should keep you going for a while,"

"Wonderful George," said Tony.

Colonel Stewart then reached below his seat and produced a silver platter with a pie tied to it by a red ribbon while everyone applauded except Tony.

George went on, "We thought we'd use this moment to officially unveil Mrs Blair's pies as the official meat pastry of the *Humans to Mars* Mission. You must be so pleased."

"Yes George," said Tony. "Fantastic."

"Well Blair," said George, "the media boys down here would love a shot of you eating a mouthful or two. Do you think you could manage a bit now for us all back here on Earth?"

I'm going to be sick on camera, thought Tony who had actually been quite hungry. "Yes George."

Stewart carried the pie over to him and untied the ribbon. Reluctantly, Tony picked up the pie and brought it to his lips while Siberry starting recording the event on a camera. Tony could already smell the nasty chemical taste in the pastry. Very slowly, he opened his mouth and bit down on the crust meeting the cold, grey, dead animal matter inside. "Mmm, er, delicious," he said almost gagging whilst everyone else clapped again.

"And cut!" said Siberry.

Tony gave the platter to Marshall and turned away to retch.

"Er, sorry Tony," said Siberry, "but the lens cap was still on. Can you do that again please?"

Tony said nothing. Reluctantly, he received the platter back from Marshall and felt a discontented rumbling coming from his stomach.

"There's a good boy," said George from a far-off place.

II

Deep Space Tony

"...*and I say, you're the future now. Make what you..."*
Click. Tony stopped the video clip, lay back on his pillow and closed his eyes. At the time he'd wanted to say *you'll be begging me to come back one day* but his team of advisors wouldn't let him. Watching old videos of himself was how he'd filled most of the seemingly-endless time since leaving Earth *God-knows* how long ago.

What to do now though? he thought with a deep sigh. He opened his eyes and gazed once more at the worn and creased photograph above his head. *Oh George*, thought Tony, *love won't tear us apart again.* Disappointingly, George had only contacted the orbiter once during the entire journey. On the many occasions Tony had contacted Earth to try to speak with him, Mission Control had said that George was either in a meeting, on holiday, in the shower, had laryngitis or was just simply unavailable. *Oh George*, he thought adoringly, *ever the hard-worker.*

Feeling inspired by George's work ethic, Tony decided to read his emails. Sadly, there was nothing from George but there was however, a dispatch from his beloved wife Cherie which he opened without much enthusiasm. According to the message she had started divorce proceedings against him and was going to marry Boris Zhirkhov when their separation became official. For a moment Tony thought about how they had met, the four children they had conceived and their subsequent life together. *Good riddance really*, he thought philosophically. *He's welcome to her. It's George I love.* He then noticed that Selwyn Corbett had also sent him a message.

Tony, I know it's been a while but how soon can you get back? I've spoken to an insider at Channel 5 and they reckon that The Shining will definitely happen and get this – forget Grady – they want to audition you for Torrance x

Tony replied with the words *stall them 'til I get back* and then with a sigh removed a paperback from the drawer near his pillow. He stared at the picture of Jack Nicholson going mad on the front cover and wondered if there was an axe anywhere onboard the *McDonald*. Deciding to make a start on the *bleedin' thing* now before their arrival on Mars, he opened the first page.

Stephen King was born in Portland, Maine…

Just then the face of Colonel Siberry appeared on the video screen near his head. "Hi Tony, good news, we've actually arrived. We are now orbiting the Red Planet."

"Er, right," said Tony, "er, great."

"James wants everyone down on the bridge to discuss where we go from here. There's also a group message due to arrive from NASA."

"Oh, I'd love to," said Tony, "but my foot is really aching and, er…"

"Oh Tony," said Siberry, giving him a wink, "perhaps you'd like me to come down there and rub it better for you?"

"Er, I'm on my way now," said Tony hurriedly tightening the cord of his snow leopard dressing gown.

"Quite something, ain't it, Tony?" said Chief Marshall as Tony strapped himself into his flight seat on the bridge.

"Er, yeah, wonderful." said Tony uncertainly. *All this way for that,* he thought looking at a brown-red planet through the cockpit windows.

"How's that diary of yours coming along, Tony?" asked Marshall sat to his left.

"Er, yeah, great," said Tony who had recently agreed to repay the Daily Mail his one hundred grand fee.

"Almost there with that transmission," said Siberry from the co-pilot's seat.

The pilot turned around to face Tony. "Remember Tony," said a smiling Commander Collins, "because it takes about ten minutes to receive messages now, this is a recorded video, so it's pointless asking if you can go home yet or if President Bush is there."

"I knew that," said Tony.

Siberry flicked a switch on the console and the image of the mission figurehead, Rear Admiral Sayers appeared on the monitor screens above the windows. "Many greetings

McDonald from everyone here at NASA," said Sayers warmly. "I am making this call on the eve of your journey to the surface of Mars to wish you all good luck from every single person down here on Earth. Your endeavours have inspired countless millions to aspire to greater things in their lives and to reach beyond each horizon."

Peasants, thought Tony, *who cares?*

"Good luck everybody," continued Sayers. "We'll have a drink together on my flagship when you get back. Work together and you can achieve so much. I'm very proud of you all, Sayers out." The screen went blank.

"Right people," said Collins. "Alice and I have identified a touchdown window for the first landing. Storm Ares looks like it's now going to lift earlier than we anticipated and we've managed to make contact with the transponder down at the landing zone. Therefore, I'm proposing we send the pioneer group down in about twenty hours; basically, that's myself and Leonard. Then once we've set up the outer skin, we're going to start ferrying everyone else down to the surface in the *Heinz*. Anyone want to speak?"

Tony raised his hand, "Er, just that, if you need anyone to remain on board and guard the plane from any, erm, you know, well…"

"Thank you, Tony, for your kind offer," said Collins smiling at him, "but everything up here is completely automated and we need your vital expertise and assistance down on Mars. Right people, go and get some rest and we'll meet again in eighteen hours."

Oh George, thought Tony longingly, *we'll meet again, don't know where…*

III

A Day in the Life

Tony looked through the transparent plastic panels of the biome where an alien pink sky met the land at some distant hills. Lit by a pale weak Sun, a dust devil could be seen close by, dancing across an almost-flat, barren landscape. *Am I really here?* he asked himself in disbelief. *What is this dreadful place?*

"Tony, are you ready yet?" said a woman's voice from behind him.

Tony blinked, opened his mouth but no words came out. He looked upwards toward where the *McDonald*, his only way of getting home, back to George, was orbiting this alien rock. *Oh George,* he thought disconsolately *why did you send me here?*

"Tony," said the voice again, this time more insistent, "the line please."

Tony swallowed and climbed off the storage crate he

was sitting on. He tightened his dressing gown cord and turned around. "And that's why," said Tony trying hard to smile as he held a small blue box, "after a hard day out on the Martian surface searching for extra-terrestrial life, I turn to *Ache-o-kill Plus*, the official non-prescription analgesic of the *Humans to Mars* Mission to take away those pains."

"Cut!" said Colonel Siberry smiling at him. "Well done Tony, I think you're getting better. You know something, I just love your British accent."

"Ahem," said Tony who was getting a bit worried by all the compliments and winks he was receiving from her of late. *She's old enough to be my granny.*

"I'll do the editing now and send it off to Earth forthwith," said Siberry packing the camera into a box.

"Oh, that's great," said Tony, walking towards the sleeping areas.

"And by the way Tony…" said Siberry winking at him.

"Er, yes."

"…can you suit up and go outside please? The rig's finished drilling now and Bob needs more samples."

Bob can go and…

Tony pressed the release button for the outer doors.

It had taken ages to get the *bleedin'* surface suit on. *That'll learn them*, he thought defiantly after deliberately not checking his suit for tears, *if I don't make it back.* The doors swooshed open and he stepped out onto the surface. Steadying himself on the outside of the base, he breathed hard and looked around. *I thought Trimdon was bad, but this...* A weak breeze blew around him as he limped past where the *Heinz* was parked, towards a shiny metallic cuboid about thirty metres away from the base.

He brushed the layer of fine dust off the rig controls, pulled the release lever and a hatch at the bottom opened to reveal a bucket-full of rock ice. *Bleedin' Hell*, he thought with the effort of carrying the ice back to base.

Exhausted by now, Tony exited the air-lock and heaved the bucket into the biome where he found Chief Marshall looking through a microscope.

"Oh, well done Tony," said Marshall spotting the pail. "Bring it over please and come and have a look at this slide."

"What now?" said Tony who would rather have gone for a sleep.

"Here, have a look," said Marshall standing away from the microscope.

"What am I meant to be looking at?" said Tony looking down the lenses, "All I can see are a load of blobs."

"Those *blobs* are a kind of microbial life unique to Mars. We've discovered extra-terrestrial life, Tony. Aliens, if you will."

Is that all? thought Tony, a bit underwhelmed. "Oh yeah, er, great," he said as enthusiastically as he could, "erm, wonderful."

"There must be great lakes of liquid water under the surface of Mars..."

How nice, thought Tony wearily.

"...all kinds of microbes unknown to science. Entire ecosystems..."

"Sorry Bob," said Tony edging towards the exit, "but if you don't mind, I've, er, got to go and speak to, er, Len." Then he skipped through the flap into a darkened meeting area.

As he crept towards the sleeping areas, a soft voice from the shadows said, "Hi Tony."

Tony froze like a rabbit caught in car headlights. "Er…"

"Come over here please, Tony," said Colonel Siberry turning on a small desk light to reveal herself. "I need you to help me with these figures."

"Erm…"

"Here Tony," said Siberry holding out a piece of paper, "read out the numbers so that I can *enter* them into the computer."

"Ahem," said Tony trying not to get too close to her. Reluctantly, he took the paper and began to read, "twenty five…"

"Oh Tony," said Siberry, "why are you all the way over there? Come nearer and sit down."

Hesitantly, he came closer. "Twenty five…"

"Oh Tony," said Siberry almost in a whisper. "Did I say that I just love your British accent? I could listen to you speak all day."

Crumbs, thought Tony, now regretting telling his crewmates about his recent divorce.

"You know Tony," she said leaning ever closer to him, "my first husband, Bernard was from London. Whenever he spoke to me, I always found it hard to say *no*."

"What happened to him?" squeaked Tony, shrinking back into his seat.

"He died... ...of a heart attack." Her lips were now that close to his that he could smell the mintiness of *Firmodent*, the official denture adhesive of the *Humans to Mars* Mission on her breath.

"Oh Tony," said Siberry breathlessly, "it might just be the hormone tablets but…"

Just then the flap opened from the sleeping areas and in stepped Colonel Stewart. "I'm not disturbing anything, am I?" said a grinning Stewart.

Please not the rig. "Er, no Len," said Tony, "we were just, er…"

Stewart turned to Siberry, "Alice, I need a fresh pair of eyes to look over the reactor manual with me. The numbers coming off the fuel rods don't match what they should."

"Sure thing, Leonard," said Siberry getting up sprightly. "Let's do it."

After they'd gone Tony sighed, took a deep breath and logged on to the computer to read his emails. Happily, the spam filters were now removing all those annoying messages either about the mission or about the deceased of *long-forgotten* wars he'd been involved with. This left a single dispatch in his inbox from Mr Ho who wrote with the news that the house in Oxfordshire had been mothballed and his beloved ex-wife Cherie had moved to Moscow. The message finished by saying that Jalal had taken to hiding in the garage between pallets of festering pastries to avoid being arrested. *The poor chap just did what he had to.*

Tony sat back and realised that he wasn't really that bothered about Cherie anyway. The more he thought about it, he found that he was actually pleased that some other *sucker* had taken her off his hands. *Oh George*, he thought basking once more in the warm glow of George's love, *it's you that I love.*

Just then the face of Commander Collins appeared on the screen. "Hi Tony," smiled Collins, "the rig is ready for collection now."

Fiddlesticks! thought Tony feeling a dreadful ache in his left foot.

IV

Merry Xmas Everybody on Mars

Another one without George, thought Tony miserably as pale Martian sunshine shone through the transparent panels of the biome. He looked down at the greyish brown pastry in front of him on the table and felt his appetite rapidly dissipate.

"Happy Christmas, Tony," said Colonel Siberry to his left, holding an offering in her hand. "Would you like to my pull my *cracker*, Mr Blair?"

"Erm," he said, limply accepting the end of the cracker. *Years and years without George and now this*, he thought as Siberry placed a paper hat on his head. More upsetting was the fact that he wasn't able to hear George's silken tones wishing him *Season's Greetings* this year, nor had George's Christmas e-card arrived yet.

Just then the zipper opened from the meeting area and Commander Collins appeared carrying a tray of plastic cups. "Here you go people," said a smiling Collins placing the tray on the table. "Christmas drinks."

"What is it?" said Tony taking a cup.

"Rover fuel or should we say *Mars Gin*?" said Collins. "I reckon we can spare a bit today of all days."

"One hundred per cent pure ethanol," said a smiling Chief Marshall on Tony's right, "so go easy tiger".

Tony took a sniff and then a sip. *Crumbs!* he thought feeling his throat and tongue burning. "I've had stronger," he rasped unconvincingly.

"Cheers everyone and Merry Christmas," said Collins sitting down and raising his beaker.

"Good health people," said Colonel Stewart sitting opposite Tony.

"All the best," said Marshall.

"Bottoms up," said Siberry patting Tony's knee under the table.

Tony gave a slight flinch as he raised his cup to utter a weak, "Cheers."

"Tuck in, people," said Collins, "there's seconds as well."

Seconds? Tony took another look at the *noxious* pastry in front of him and sighed. He opened the pie lid with his knife and the aroma of the contents filled his nostrils, *like some long-extinct swamp rat.* He speared a piece of pie crust with his fork and brought it up to his mouth. The stale flour smell coupled with a nasty chemical aroma made him gag immediately and almost abandon the attempt. Slowly, he lowered the morsel into his mouth and tried to swallow it whole to avoid any tasting. "Erghh," he said as the piece got stuck in his throat.

"Oh Tony," said Siberry giving him a powerful thump on the back with her hand, "is that better?"

"Thanks," wheezed Tony. He took another swig from his cup to clear his throat and almost choked again such was the strength of the alcohol. "Excuse me," he croaked, purple-faced, getting up from his chair and fleeing into the meeting area.

"You carry on Tony," said a smiling Marshall. "We'll keep your pie for when you get back."

Not bleedin' likely, thought Tony from the safety of the meeting area. He took a deep breath to compose himself and then sat down at the computer to check for George's card, but before he could open his inbox, Colonel Siberry stepped through the flap from the biome.

"Oh Tony," said Siberry caressing her pigtails. "I was starting to get a bit worried about you."

"Oh, I'm fine now," said Tony nervously. "In fact, I'm better than fine. I was just on my way back…"

"Listen Tony," said Siberry approaching his chair. "There's something I've been meaning to talk to you about."

Please, thought Tony desperately, *not another foot-rub!*

"When I met you all those years ago, I thought you were a bit of a showboater, but now I've come to like you…" She sat down next to him and touched the back of his hand.

"Er…"

"…and maybe we should start getting to know each other a little better."

"Oh, you know, erm," he said pulling his hand back, "I'm still a bit upset about my Cherie and all that."

"It's alright Tony," she said leaning closer, "I understand completely. My third husband, Bill, never came back from Vietnam. It took me days to get over it."

"How did he die?" squeaked Tony.

"Oh, he wasn't killed. He absconded with a hooker he'd met in Bangkok."

Lucky bleeder. "I'm really sorry about that but…"

"I'm not and you know why, *Mr Blair*?"

"Er, no…"

"Because Tony, a woman has *needs*."

"Erm, can you just give me a couple of months to think about it?"

"Oh Tony, you're such a tease. I'm going back to sit with the others now you seem a little better, but maybe I'll see you later," said Siberry winking at him as she left.

When she had gone Tony sighed with relief and opened his inbox on the computer. Sadly, there was still no sign of George's Christmas e-card which was disappointing as Tony had also wanted to hear George's opinion of his idea for a new family-breakdown talk-show to be called *Your Dilemma on Telly* which Tony would host. There was however, a message from Selwyn Corbett.

Tony old boy, sorry it's bad news. I'm afraid the part of Torrance has gone south. The rumours are that Michael McIntyre is a shoo-in. I'm still working to get you on the next Strictly so don't worry, something will crop up x

Tony sighed at this fresh disappointment and focussed his mind on the only thing that he cared for anymore: George's love. He closed his eyes and could see himself with George dancing a waltz together around a glitzy ballroom. *Oh George,* he thought, *lead on, mon amour.*

V
The Pies of Wrath

Tony wiped the dust from his gloves and pulled down the Polaroid visor on his helmet. It was early afternoon out on the surface of Mars and his temperature wrist gauge was reading 39 Fahrenheit. *Oh happy day*, he thought basking in the faint Martian sunshine.

Today, just outside the Mars Base, a funeral was about to break out. Tony loved funerals. Perhaps the greatest regret of his life was that he hadn't attended Gordon's send-off yet. Tony had gone through his head many times what he was going to say from the graveside on that joyous occasion.

…comrades from the party, members of the press. Gordon was my inspiration, my rock, my everything…

His reveries were disturbed by his fellow crewmates firing their handguns as a mark of respect to the deceased. Tony was feeling a bit *miffed* that *he*, former prime minister

Tony Blair hadn't been given a firearm. He recalled the time on Surtsey when he almost killed the weapons course leader with a stray round which had then ricocheted off a rock and hit himself in the lower leg. The accident and subsequent time-off to recover had almost cost him his place on the mission. Fortunately, George had intervened yet again to make sure that he didn't miss out on going to Mars, by sending his own doctor to discharge Tony from the hospital early. *Good old George*, thought Tony nostalgically, *always looking out for me.*

This morning at around seven forty five, Chief Engineer Marshall had been found dead in his quarters by Colonel Siberry. Normally a vegetarian, Marshall had eaten his first *Mrs Blair's* pie the night before to help prolong the other rations. Siberry had since pronounced him having died in his sleep of natural causes.

Those evil pies have claimed another victim, thought Tony recalling the mask of terror frozen on to Marshall's face before his interment. *At least he's not suffering anymore, unlike me.* Tony had been looking forward to having the quarters he'd shared with Marshall all to himself, but had just received the unwelcome news that Colonel Stewart had become his new sleeping *buddy* to give Commander Collins more room.

"Goodbye Bob," said Stewart placing a wooden cross on Marshall's cairn, "ashes to ashes…"

Fun to funky, sang Tony in his head, *I know Major…* When he'd been prime minister, Tony being a huge David Bowie fan, had repeatedly invited the singer over to Number Ten to discuss the two of them forming a band and releasing an album together. Each time though, Bowie's manager had said that David was *too busy* and couldn't make it. Towards the end of Tony's tenure in Downing Street, Bowie, *the miserable swine*, had even refused to sing at a birthday party that Tony had been organising for an Australian friend.

"...dust to dust. He was a good fellow, Robert Marshall," said Stewart with tears in his eyes. "Damned visor's steaming up. Does anyone want to say anything?"

Tony piped up, "I lent him twenty dollars back on Earth. Can I have a look through his things for it?"

"Oh, just do what you want, Blair," said Stewart angrily.

After the funeral, Tony had a good rummage through Marshall's possessions in their shared quarters. He binned all the photographs he found and then discovered an old Hawaiian-style shirt covered with images of palm trees that Marshall had said originally belonged to Jack Lord whom he claimed to have known well.

"De, de, de-de, der, derr, de, de, de-de, derr," hummed Tony as he put the shirt on. He lay back in his bunk, closed his eyes and could see himself in Honolulu with George, crusading together against organised crime. *Oh George*, he thought dreamily, *my Dano to your McGarrett*.

Just then the zipper opened from the meeting area next door. Tony froze immediately and pretended to be asleep.

"Tony?" said a man's voice.

Please not the rig.

"Come on, Tony," said the voice sternly, "wake up."

"Uh, oh," said Tony, opening his eyes to see the white-haired figure of Colonel Stewart sitting on the opposite bunk, "Er, I was just…"

Stewart smiled at him and said, "Look Tony, I know that science and technology are not your strongest areas but we want you to take over Bob's role as science officer."

Gosh, thought Tony, *a job at last!* "Er, okie dokie."

Stewart continued, "Have a look through Bob's documents on the computer and try and pick up where he left off. Bob was also in charge of respirator maintenance. If you need any help just ask me, James or Alice."

"Right-ee-oh."

"Oh, and Tony…"

"Yes Len?"

"…the rig should be ready by now."

Fiddlesticks!

An hour or so later Tony found himself back outside on the Martian surface. Being sent out to get more ice wasn't all bad he reasoned as he limped towards the rig. After all, he could just take his time on the task and focus his mind on the real inspiration in his life, George. *Oh George*, he thought as he opened the ice hatch, *your struggle is our struggle.*

He headed back to the base with the bucket but as he was passing the *Heinz*, a high-pitched whining sound filled the inside of his helmet. He recalled from his mission training that it was a warning but couldn't quite remember what for. Thankfully, when he gave the helmet a sharp rap with his hand, the *bleedin'* noise stopped. He carried on but as he neared the air-lock doors he began to struggle to breathe. Then he realised what the warning meant: his surface suit had been pierced or torn and his air supply was running low. Immediately, he dropped the bucket and began checking for holes. *Crumbs*, he thought finding a large rip below his right arm.

Much to his relief, he made it to the outer doors without dying but when he pressed the entry button, the doors didn't budge. In despair, he banged on the button panel with his fist but still nothing happened. *Oh George*, he thought, leaning on the entrance, *c'est la mort*. Then, whether it was the pressure from his body or the delayed response of the electronics, the doors parted and he fell into the air-lock, landing in a heap on the floor.

In the biome he found Colonel Siberry on her own watering tomato seedlings. "Hi Tony," she said as he staggered out of the air-lock. "You've been a while."

"The outer doors…" gasped a red-faced Tony.

"Yes?"

"…stuck…"

"Oh dear, it must be the dust," said Siberry nonchalantly. "It's playing havoc with all the exposed electronics. I'll mention it to Leonard."

"Er, yes, great," said Tony inching towards the sleeping areas.

"Tony," said Siberry, "why don't you come over here and help me water these plants."

"Er, no thanks, erm, I've got to go and erm… have there been any messages from Earth?"

"Nothing major."

"Oh well," said Tony, "must dash."

"Wait a minute, Tony," said Siberry touching his arm as he passed, "you'll never guess the surprise I've got for you this evening."

Please no more old scars. "Er, yes?" said Tony nervously.

Siberry reached down to the floor and brought up a blue plastic bottle with the words NOT FOR HUMAN CONSUMPTION written on the side. "Mars Gin? James has said it's okay if we have a few tonight," she said with a wink.

"Oh, erm, I've still got that terrible headache, I'm afraid."

"Oh Tony," said Siberry taking his hand, "are you still feeling bad about your ex-wife?"

"Bearing up, I suppose."

"You know, you have such soft palms."

You won't be thinking that when they're wrapped around your... "Sorry, but, er, I've got to go and talk to, er," he said pulling away.

"Oh, alright then," said Siberry, "maybe later then, *Mr Blair.*"

Not bleedin' likely. "Yeah bye," said Tony skipping through the flap into next door. In reality, he had no intention of speaking with anyone. He went directly to his quarters and lay down on his bunk. As he drifted off to sleep, he gazed at the photograph near his pillow and felt George's guiding presence close by. *Oh, George,* he thought sleepily, *who needs women when I've got your love.*

That night, Tony was awoken by the sound of a zipper

opening. It was very dark in his quarters but he could just about make out a shadowy figure removing its clothing.

Old Len's not a bad old sort really, he thought as the world of dreams began to take him once more. He was almost back at George's ranch when he felt a hand move across the outside of his sleeping bag and touch him on the foot.

"Tony," whispered Siberry softly in his ear, "I thought you might like some company tonight, so I've swapped with Leonard. Budge over."

Yikes, thought Tony, as he felt the hand move over his leg. All he could do was to keep tight hold of the zipper at the top of the sleeping bag and think hard about Texas.

VI

Day Tripper

"Get away Gordon!" said Tony fighting shadows. "You'll never be prime minister of Mars."

"Tony," said a man's voice.

"Close the windows of the shuttle, Cherie."

"Wake up Tony, you're dreaming."

"George?"

"No, it's me, Collins."

Tony opened his eyes and lifted his head to see the mission commander smiling at him from the bunk opposite. He blinked and looked around his quarters having had the strangest of dreams last night...

"Morning Tony," said Collins. "I'm going outside today to collect some geological samples and I want you to come with me."

"What time is it now?" asked Tony blearily.

"It's ten twenty."

"Er, wouldn't it best if I stayed and guarded the base from, er, or in case the central heating plays up or something?"

"As you're science officer now, I must ask you kindly to come along. I thought we'd use the rover to explore a series of parallel gullies and ridges about ten clicks from here. Then on the way back, there's an extinct volcano we can check out…"

Boring, thought Tony feeling his eyelids becoming heavy again.

Tony yawned. He was standing in the air-lock feeling like it was much too early to be out of bed.

"I think that's all the checks," said Commander Collins smiling at him. "You ready Tony?"

I couldn't be worse. "Er, check."

"Okay, let's roll," said Collins dropping his Polaroid visor and pressing the exit button.

Science officer, thought Tony proudly, feeling a bit like the old Tony again, who once upon a time had fêted princes and presidents alike from the sofa in his den in Downing Street, not like the despised, craven figure he felt he had become since being deposed by Gordon. *Gosh*, he thought as the door swooshed open, *I guess it really is something to be on another planet.*

Tony followed Collins out to where the rover, *Argos* was parked a short distance away. *At least it's not that wretched Prius,* thought Tony climbing into the passenger seat whilst Collins cleaned the dust off the windscreen.

"Belt up," said Collins starting the rover. As they bounced along the rocky Martian surface, Tony gazed out through the perspex at the alien landscape in front of him, and thought about George and how wonderful he was. He remembered the times he'd visited George's ranch in Texas, the happiest times of his life and how George always seemed to have a nice surprise waiting for him there. All his doubts and concerns about being sent to Mars seemed to vanish through the lens of George's love. Soon the bouncing motion of the rover began to make him rather sleepy.

...ladies and gentlemen, members of the Presidential Committee. Thank you for the National Medal of Science. First of all, I'd like to dedicate this award to...

Tony, roared the crowd of dignitaries from the White House lawn.

"Wake up Tony," said Collins shaking him gently on the shoulder. "We've reached our first locality."

Tony opened his eyes, yawned and looked at his watch. "Have you got the time, Jim?" he asked shaking his wrist.

"It's thirteen fifty," said Collins getting out of the rover. "*Gee whizz* Tony," he declaimed looking out over the Martian landscape, "this place sure beats 'Nam."

For the next hour Tony and Commander Collins took photographs, collected rock samples and surveyed the topography. *At least*, thought Tony, putting small pieces of rock into a polythene bag, *we're not making some ghastly commercial.*

Then it was time for lunch. Tony sat with Collins on a small hillock. Between slurps of liquidised pie through a tube, they talked about each other's past. Collins showed

Tony a picture of his Vietnamese wife and daughter from his days as a prisoner-of-war. "I was in that labour camp for twenty seven years, you know Tony."

Tony then reciprocated the gesture with the photograph of himself and George in Texas.

"Were you and President Bush close buddies back on Earth, Tony?" asked Collins.

"Oh well, you know…" said Tony coyly, going red in the cheeks.

"Come on then, Tony," said Collins patting him on the shoulder, "let's get back in the rover and go to our next site."

"Are you coming, Tony?" said Collins from the lip of a large caldera.

"Erm, I'll stay and er, guard the rover just in case, er…" said Tony.

"Okay, I want you to keep track of time as my suit chronometer is playing up. We've only got about an hour of oxygen left so I want you to radio me when thirty minutes have passed."

"Er, check," said Tony watching Stewart disappear over the crater edge. Then he reclined his seat, closed his eyes and contemplated the important things in his life. *Oh George,* he thought feeling George's protective spirit envelop him once more, *we were with you at the first, we will stay with you to the end.*

Soon enough he was back in the House of Commons during PM's Questions,

"*…and I say every time I am asked, I remain confident that they will be found…*"

"Tony," said his chancellor seated next to him.
"Not now, can't you see I'm busy?"
"Tony?" but this time it wasn't Gordon.
"What?"
"I said, *Collins here*," said a voice from inside his helmet. "How much time have we got left, Tony?"
"Oh, erm, loads of time…" said Tony looking at his watch which read ten minutes to two. He then noticed that the second hand was static. "… but, er, I think you'd better come back right now."
"Why? How much longer is there?"
"Er, that's the thirty minutes up now," said Tony shaking his wrist furiously.

Later that evening, Tony got out of his bunk and tightened his dressing gown cord. He stuck his head into the meeting area and when he was sure that it was empty, crept inside. He logged on to the computer in order to ask Selwyn Corbett if he could put him forward as a presenter of a programme like *Tomorrow's World* or *Horizon* now that he was such an expert on space and all things scientific.

Dear Selwyn…

Just then the zipper from the biome opened and in stepped Commander Collins. "Tony, there you are" said Collins cheerily, walking over towards him.

Please not the rig. "Er, yes Jim?"

"I've just checked our respirators from today," said Collins patting him on the shoulder, "and I've never seen two as empty as those."

"Er…"

"Make sure you get that watch sorted out, buddy. By the way, Leonard and I are venturing outside tomorrow at eight hundred hours to investigate the eastern edge of Valles Marineris..."

Boring.

"...and we need two respirators filling for the journey. Would you mind, Tony?"

Oh why me? "Er, check," said Tony.

"I'm off to get some shut-eye now," said Collins. "Oh, one more thing…"

Please not the rig.

"…Alice was looking for you earlier. She said that she would be in her quarters all night and you're welcome to join her for a few drinks."

"Er…"

"Tony, you old dog," said Collins ruffling his hair and laughing as he left for the sleeping areas.

Tony hurriedly finished sending the email to Selwyn Corbett and then fled to the biome where it was easier to hide.

After he'd filled two respirators, he lay down on a coir mat between the rows of potato plants and gazed at the image of himself with George in Texas taken all those years ago. George's radiant eyes gazed into his and he knew that no force in the Universe could prevent their eventual reunion. *Oh George*, thought Tony, feeling himself almost back in Texas, *thy will be done.*

VII

Two Funerals and a Wedding

… ladies and gentlemen, fellow peace-lovers…

Tony, roared the audience in adulation.

… thank you so much for this Gandhi Peace Award. I'd like to mention one person in particular…

"Tony, wake up," said a woman's voice.
"Oh George," said Tony.
"No, it's me, Alice."
"Where am I?" he said opening his eyes to see Colonel Siberry stood over him.
"You're in the biome. You must have fallen asleep in here last night"
"What time is it?"

"Time to get up; we've got a potential emergency on our hands."

"Please not the rig…"

"No, James and Leonard have gone missing."

Crumbs!

According to Siberry, Commander Collins and Colonel Stewart had set off earlier that morning in fine spirits but no contact had been received or made with them since and that was more than three hours ago. Stewart had sent a final radio message an hour after leaving which no one on the base had picked up at the time. He sounded very distressed on the recording, "Can… hardly… breathe… anymore… send help…Crater 7…urgh…"

Tony remembered filling the respirators last night but was a bit unsure as to whether or not he'd checked to see if they were empty prior to refilling them. Distant voices kept saying something about *unused gases…*

Better keep quiet about that one, Tony old chap, thought Tony as he stood in the air-lock about to embark upon the rescue mission.

"It may just be that their radios have malfunctioned," said Colonel Siberry standing next to him, "but we'll have to go and look for them in any case."

"Erm, maybe it would be better if I stayed behind on the base in order to conserve oxygen and er, to man the radio just in case they get in…" said Tony stepping back towards the biome doors.

"Oh Tony," said Siberry touching his arm, "I promise I'll be gentle with you."

"Er…"

"Okay Tony, I want you to check my suit for any holes. Make sure that you feel in all the crevices."

Is this really happening to me? thought Tony, trying to make as little contact as possible with any of her crevices.

"Oh Tony, you have such gentle hands," said Siberry speaking softly close to his ear. "Right my turn now. Lift your arms up and spread your legs apart."

"Oh look at the time…" said Tony side-stepping away from her. "Er, isn't it getting a bit late to go now?"

"Don't worry Tony," said Siberry pressing the exit button. "It's only eleven thirty so there'll be plenty of daylight for us to get out and back in."

"But I've got this awful ache in my foot."

"Perhaps you'd like me to massage it for you now before we set off proper," said Siberry reaching down.

"Er, no thanks," said Tony stepping back, "I'm sure it'll be fine, really."

The outer doors swooshed open and Tony gestured for Siberry to go first.

"Oh Tony," said Siberry breathlessly, "you're so gallant."

Siberry led the way and they headed south east. After twenty minutes she called a halt near a sunlit gully where Tony lay down in the red sand with exhaustion. Siberry climbed a narrow ridge, looked at her wrist tracking device and said, "I've got a reading on the rover due south. It's not far at all."

Not far? thought Tony with disbelief. He stared up at the pink sky and wondered if his life could get any worse.

Oh George, he thought despairingly, *why am I here in this terrible place?*

"Come on Tony," said Siberry offering him her hand. She helped him up and they carried on, Siberry in front, Tony limping along some distance behind.

Ten minutes later, they found the rover parked at the bottom of a rocky escarpment but there was no sign of either Collins or Stewart. Tony breathing heavily, went and sat down in the *Argos* whilst Siberry checked the engine out.

"The rover seems fine," said Siberry sitting down next to him. "I think I've located where James and Leonard are from their short-range trackers." She pointed over to the right. "It looks like they're over there in that canyon."

"You go…" said a weary-sounding Tony.

"Oh Tony," said Siberry turning towards him, "perhaps, you'd like me to check your suit for any holes again. The crotch area is notoriously…"

"Er, no thanks," said Tony leaping out of the vehicle, "I'm sure it's fine. Let's go now."

"Oh Tony," said Siberry, "I love it when you tell me what to do."

Go and…

From the edge of the canyon Siberry removed a small pair of binoculars from her pocket. "I think I can see one of them. Let's go Tony," she said grabbing his hand, "just a little bit further now."

They found the bodies at the bottom of the canyon, Stewart first and then Collins a bit further along, both stone dead. Exhausted, Tony slumped to the ground while Siberry examined the corpses.

"I can't see any outward signs of causes of death," said Siberry when she'd finished looking over the bodies. "With this slope, there's no way we'd get the rover out of here. I guess we're just going to have to leave them here and cover them with rocks like we did for old Bob. Come on Tony, start collecting."

Fiddlesticks.

After half an hour, a pile of stones covered each body. Tony, who had never felt so spent, lay prostrate on the ground staring up at the pale Sun. *Oh George*, he thought almost bereft of any hope, *you are my sunshine…*

"That should do it. Here Tony, get up," said Siberry helping him up again. "Do you want to say anything?"

"Erm," said Tony, "have you got the right time? This *bleedin'* watch keeps …"

"It's three thirty."

Siberry then said a short poem by the graveside in honour of the deceased.

Poets, thought Tony adjusting his watch, *how many standing ovations have they ever had?*

"Tony, do you know what date it is today?" said Siberry throwing some sand on Stewart's cairn.

"Er, sometime in February?"

"Yes, it's the 29th."

"And?"

"Well, traditionally it's the day ladies can ask their gentlemen to marry them."

"Surely, you're not…"

"Oh Tony, will you marry me please?"

"Er, I'd, erm, love to but I'm still cut up about my Cherie. She, er, was my rock, you know."

"I understand Tony," said Siberry producing a gold ring from her chest pocket, "but there's no time like the present and time is short."

"Erm," said Tony desperately, "er, wouldn't it be better to wait at least until we got back to the base?"

"Come on Tony," she said taking his arm, "you can be the best man as well as the groom. I'll guide you through it.

"Do you Tony, take this woman Alice to be your lawfully wedded wife?"

Tony didn't know what to say. He knew he certainly didn't want to say *yes* but somehow couldn't bring himself to say *no*. "Er…"

"Come on Tony, just nod your head," said Siberry pressing the ring into his hand.

Languidly, he moved his head up and down once and then Siberry guided his fingers to give her back the ring.

"By the powers granted to me by Almighty God, NASA and the United States Air Force, I now declare us man and wife. You may now kiss the bride." Siberry then grabbed hold of his shoulders and pressed her visor against his. Tony almost passed out through shock and had to lie down on the ground again. When he had recovered, he found Siberry sitting next to him. "Come on then, let's head back." she said winking at him. "I've got a *special surprise* for you later at the base, *Mr Blair*."

Perhaps, thought Tony with a grimace, *it's just a game of Scrabble.*

Tony awoke in the darkness and looked at his watch which said the time was three thirty. As he shook his wrist, the events of the previous day hit him like a huge instalment of bad news. *Far too frisky for someone so old*, he thought with a shudder.

Fortunately, his memory was somewhat dulled by the copious amounts of Mars Gin he'd imbibed on returning to the base. *I probably imagined most of it*, he thought trying to reassure himself, but when he rolled on to his side he realised that much to his horror, a sleeping Colonel Siberry was lying next to him. *Crumbs!* he thought lifting up the sleeping bag, *she's got no clothes on. And neither have I!* Moving as slowly as he could, he sat up and swung his legs out of the bunk but before he could reach for his dressing gown, a hand grabbed hold of his arm and pulled him back into bed.

"Last night was so wonderful, Mr Blair," whispered Siberry softly in his ear.

Last night? thought Tony utterly aghast.

"Oh Tony, what stamina you have."

Stamina? "Er, what time is it?" he squeaked trying to get up.

"It's time," said Siberry rolling over towards him, "for a repeat performance."

Yikes!

VIII
A Single Man

*A*nthony *Charles Lynton Blair*, said the Archbishop of Canterbury, *do you take this man to be your lawfully wedded...*

Tony awoke in his quarters with a dry mouth and a sore head full of dubious memories. *Oh George*, he thought despondently, *I do*. He turned to his left and realised the events of last night weren't just a bad dream after all. Colonel Siberry or *Mrs Blair* as she was calling herself now, was indeed lying next to him. *It's the varicose veins that I can't abide,* he thought with a shiver. He gently touched her shoulder and on getting no response, quietly got up, put on his dressing gown and slowly unzipped the exit flap.

In the meeting area he logged on to the computer and a welcome email from George helped ease his troubles, even though it was the same message as always. *Oh George*, thought Tony admiringly, *how do you find the time to be so great?*

Then he blinked with excitement when he noticed there was a message from his agent. Maybe, this was that big opportunity that he knew would eventually happen. With some trepidation he opened the email.

Hi Tony, sorry but there's no interest from anyone here about your science angle and it's bad news about Strictly – it's full for the foreseeable but I am working at a possible guest appearance on The One Show when you get back, x

When was that again? thought Tony holding his head in his hands as the weight of the situation hit him hard. Troubling thoughts began to assail his mind. *Why, oh why did I ever send in the troops?* He remembered how getting Her Majesty to sign the deployment order had given him such a happy feeling at the time, but now given his current predicament, he wondered whether it had really been such a great idea. And why, *oh why* had he ever stepped down for that *Scottish weasel?*

As he struggled to control his feelings, he thought about George and how great he was. From his pocket he found the faded photo of himself with George in Texas, standing together, cheek by jowl against evil. George's heroic gaze made him realise that as long as George was still there for him, he didn't really need anybody else. He could almost hear George's warm, encouraging voice, something that made him feel like he could accomplish anything. *Oh George*, he thought wiping away a tear, *je t'aime.*

Later that day, Tony crept back into his quarters to find Colonel Siberry lying in the same position she had been in earlier. He'd decided it was time for a Mars Gin but the bottle was in a locked cupboard in the biome and *Mrs Blair* had the only key around her neck.

"Alice?" he said peering over the top of her head.

There was no reply but fearing a trick, he patted her on the shoulder which elicited no response. Cautiously, he reached out to take the lanyard from around her neck but as he touched her skin, he was struck by how chilly she felt. *Another one down,* he thought feeling her clammy brow. Then he removed the chemical store key from around her neck and after pulling up the sleeping bag to cover her still-smiling face, left for the biome to make himself a drink to celebrate.

Three parts powdered orange, two parts Mars Gin, one part water, he thought mantra-like as he poured the ingredients into a beaker and stirred them together with a screwdriver, a mixture he'd christened the *Tony*, the official all-day cocktail of the *Humans to Mars* Mission. "Shaken not stirred, Moneypenny," he crooned as he sat down atop of a storage crate to view the Martian landscape. *Oh George*, he thought watching an electrical storm moving over some distant hills, *no regrets*.

IX

Mars ain't the kind of Place to raise your Spirits

"How did you manage it this time, Blair?" said a palpably enraged Brian Wallace in reply to the message Tony had sent to Earth informing NASA that he was now the sole surviving crew member. "And another thing…"

Click. Tony turned the video off having heard enough of Brian's *loose* tone. *Gosh*, he thought, somewhat taken aback by the telling-off he'd just endured. How dare that man accuse him, *Tony* of what practically amounted to sabotage. *How many award nominations has he ever had?* Wallace had also said that it was impossible for any single crew member, but especially him, to fly the *Heinz* back to the *McDonald* in orbit around Mars and from there return to Earth. At least, NASA was going to fast-track the sponsorship programme in order to fund a rescue mission.

How long was that going to take again? he thought as he dragged the body of Colonel Siberry into the air-lock by her feet. It had been a week since she had died but Tony had been reluctant to deal with her corpse because he couldn't be bothered. Lately though, she was starting to give off an unpleasant odour in his quarters, so he moved her body into the biome this morning.

He pressed the exit button and the outer airlock doors swooshed open. A weak breeze blew fine dust at his visor as he hauled her over to near where Chief Engineer Marshall lay. After getting his breath back, he covered *Mrs Blair* with a few stones and then paused at the graveside. *The prime minister of Mars,* he thought proudly. He reflected that being all alone on Mars wasn't such a bad thing. There was nobody to tell him when to get up, nobody to give him any pointless tasks, no ridiculous advertisements to make, no more oversexed octogenarians to placate. *Gordon'll never steal this one from me.* All he needed to do now was to await rescue, check his emails and think about more important things than how the rig worked.

Oh George, he thought happily from the graveside, *thine is the kingdom.*

Later that day, whilst nursing a large Tony, Tony logged in to his emails hoping to hear from George about what he thought about Tony's recent idea for a new impressions show to be called *Your Boots, your Clothes and your Motorcycle* starring himself. Sadly, there were no messages from George, nothing from Selwyn Corbett, nothing even from Mr Ho. There was however, something from the *Base Mainframe* saying that the nuclear reactor had malfunctioned and all base systems were now running on emergency battery power. The message went on to say that the batteries could not be expected to last any longer than thirty hours and finished by advising immediate evacuation of the base.

Computers, thought Tony sinking his drink in one, *how many peace treaties have they ever signed?*

X
Achilles' Last Stand

Tony rubbed his eyes as he awoke into the gloom with a siren ringing too loudly to ignore. He stood up and found that the odour in his sleeping quarters was much improved now that *Mrs Blair* was *sleeping* outside. Feeling how cold it was, he donned his snow leopard dressing gown and snakeskin slippers, and fumbled his way through the dark towards the exit. *Crumbs,* thought Tony struggling to find the zipper, *I hope we brought some candles with us,* fondly recalling his time at university in the 1970s when the electricity would cut out in the halls of residence, because of the striking miners and he would have to send one of the poorer students down to the corner shop to get some tealights.

In the meeting area, much to his relief he found the computer was working but his personal account was still inaccessible. There was another message from the *Base*

Mainframe saying that because of a worsening battery situation, power was now restricted to the oxygen fans, the computer system and the air-lock doors. It foretold the power would run out in just over an hour and recommended immediate evacuation. *Crumbs*, thought Tony shivering in the cold, *I could murder a Tony right now.*

Tightening his dressing gown cord, he left for the biome where he made himself a drink with the last of the rover fuel. Then he lay down on some coir matting from where he could see the Sun rising above the distant hills which he knew was a sign of better times ahead. From his dressing gown pocket, he removed the ragged Polaroid and gazed once more upon the image taken back in Texas all those years ago. He closed his eyes and realised that it didn't matter that he was all alone on another world as he could endure anything when he had the love of one man. *Oh George*, he thought, all his doubts evaporating, *absolutely anything.*

Some time later, Tony awoke in darkness. He sat up, rubbed the ice crystals off his brow and noticed how unusually quiet it was in the biome. He rubbed his hands together and coughed. Even though he couldn't feel his fingers and toes, strangely enough, he could sense a warm glow inside of him and he knew that it meant George's guardian spirit was close by.

Then, despite the dimness in the biome, he spotted a dark object lying amongst some dying tomato plants. He stood up, tightened his dressing gown cord and retrieved the paperback from where he'd thrown it last week. He held the book in both hands and stared at the image of Jack Nicholson on the front cover. *This is it*, he thought opening the first page, determined to at least start the *bleedin' thing* after all this time.

Stephen King was born in Portland, Maine in

He got no further because all of a sudden, George appeared in the biome. "Yo Blair," said George cheerily, "how's it going, buddy?"

"Oh George," said Tony dropping the book, "I knew you would never abandon me."

"I just wanna say, Blair," said George, "that I'm very impressed with your work as my special ambassador and of all the prime ministers I ever met, you were by far the best; much better than that awful Brown guy."

"Thanks George," said Tony, "it means the world to hear your kind words."

"You know, Blair, it's kind of warm in here. I think I'm gonna take off my coat."

"Oh *moi aussi*," said Tony taking off his dressing gown, leaving on only his Union Jack underpants and Chief Marshall's Hawaiian shirt. "Are we leaving soon, George?"

"We're just waiting for the good old space boys outside to refuel the lander then we'll be off. Just sit tight. First thing we'll do when we get back is go fishing."

"Thanks again, George."

"Oh, and Blair," said George, "one more thing…"

Tony knew at this very moment that George was about to say that he loved him. The warm glow inside him intensified but it didn't matter. In fact, nothing mattered anymore, other than that George was here right now.

Oh George, thought Tony with more joy in his heart than he'd ever known before, *thank you so very much for sending me to Mars.*

Epilogue

The Texan Sun beat down remorselessly.

"Sorry George," said Tony, wiping the sweat off his brow with the back of his hand, "you were about to say something."

George didn't reply as he'd just felt something bite on his fishing line.

"You know George," said Tony, "whatever you decide, I'm…"

"Do you think, Blair," said George sounding tense, "you could just keep it for a moment?"

Tony replaced his hat on his head and then glanced left to see a dark-haired woman almost upon them. *On cue for a change.*

"Well Tony," said his beloved wife Cherie sharply, holding a camera in her hand.

"What's going on?" said George turning on his stool with surprise, causing the fishing reel to spin uncontrollably in his hands. He stood up and threw the rod away. "Goddamn it Blair, I've been trying to land that catfish for weeks."

"Er sorry George," said Tony, "but erm, I was wondering if you wouldn't mind posing for a quick snap."

"What?" said George throwing his arms about with rage. "You know I don't do unofficial photos, and besides, she shouldn't be out here. VIPs only."

"It'll take just a second, George," said Tony who could hear a helicopter getting nearer.

"I don't know, Blair. My advisors…" George stopped speaking and took a good look at the fishing hat Tony was wearing. "Hey, that belonged to my grandaddy."

"For old time's sake, eh George?" said Tony putting his arm around George's shoulders while Cherie took aim. She pressed the shutter release and then handed the camera to Tony.

As Cherie was flown away by the Secret Service, Tony watched George's manly features develop on the paper. "Oh George," he said going weak at the knees, "you know, we make such a great team together."

George didn't reply.

"George?" said Tony looking up. He scanned around and saw no one else close by. Far off in the distance, towards the main house was a figure that could have been George.

Oh George, thought Tony returning back to the image in his hand, *mission accomplished.*

For exclusive discounts on Matador titles,
sign up to our occasional newsletter at
troubador.co.uk/bookshop